Praise for

The Invisible Hand

"With *The Invisible Hand,* Ayad Akhtar solidifies the reputation he forged with *Disgraced* as a first-rate writer of fierce, well-crafted dramas that employ topicality but are not limited by it.... The prime theme is pulsing and alive: when human lives become just one more commodity to be traded, blood eventually flows in the streets."

—Brendan Lemon, *Financial Times*

"Raises probing questions about the roots of the Islamic terrorism that has rattled the world for the last decade and more."

—Charles Isherwood, *New York Times*

"A hand-wringing, throat-clenching thriller...that grabs you and won't let go."　　　　　　　　　　—Jesse Green, *New York*

"Confirms the Pakistani-American playwright as one of the theater's most original, exciting new voices.... In this tight, plot-driven thriller, Akhtar again turns hypersensitive subjects into thought-provoking and thoughtful drama. But here he also brings a grasp of money—big money—not to mention the market's unsettling connections to international politics."　　　—Linda Winer, *Newsday*

"Politically provocative.... A scary (and dreadfully funny) treatise on the universality of human greed."　　　—Marilyn Stasio, *Variety*

"A tragically contemporary thriller.... There has been precious little activity on this front since Jerry Sterner's *Other People's Money* and Caryl Churchill's *Serious Money*.... Mr. Akhtar makes up for this oversight with a vengeance."　　　—Harry Haun, *New York Observer*

"A tense, provocative thriller about the unholy nexus of international terrorism and big bucks....Akhtar...expertly decodes that vivid expression, 'blood money.'...*The Invisible Hand* jolts along like a well-made caper flick....But the taut plot is also a great setup for a fierce psychological match, and a useful colloquy on the American dollar as a force for good and evil....A very telling, compelling play." — Misha Berson, *Seattle Times*

"Whip-smart and twisty....Akhtar offers a hostage tale that balances violence, humor and geopolitical critique, never losing its edge or letting us complacently root for one side." — David Cote, *Time Out New York*

"What's the difference between a banker and a terrorist? Akhtar's new play attempts to fathom this once unfathomable question as it sounds the depths of global events, relating market 'corrections' to the logic of jihad. But *The Invisible Hand* chews on other, equally compelling questions, too: What and whose interests ultimately shape our political and moral values? Under what circumstances will we stay true to convictions — and what does it take to corrupt them?...Akhtar's musings come in the form of a suspenseful drama that could easily be a television film....*The Invisible Hand* offers genuine insight into the future of the West, and it's a brutal one to contemplate." — Tom Sellar, *Village Voice*

"*The Invisible Hand* has layers of delicious irony." — Amitava Kumar, *The Guardian*

Praise for
The Who & The What

"Disarmingly funny. A fiery...probing new play, crackling with ideas." —Charles Isherwood, *New York Times*

"At its fiercest, *The Who & The What* bares some of the same teeth as Akhtar's riveting 2013 Pulitzer-copping *Disgraced....*Akhtar's who and what are potent." —Bob Verini, *Variety*

"Vibrant. Strong and colorful. A culture-clash drama simmering with humor." —Associated Press

"A heady exploration of how one's hoped-for path in life can crash against the ramparts of family and society....*The Who & The What* helps lift a veil on a spiritual tradition that's little-portrayed on American stages. The 'what' of this ambitious play could just about fill a book by itself; the 'who' at its heart is one lively, vibrant and questioning voice." —James Hebert, *San Diego Union-Tribune*

"Fearless...powerful...Ayad Akhtar is...prodigiously talented." —Jeremy Gerard, *Deadline*

"Continually absorbing....Akhtar has a splendid command of structure, and...a fine ear for dialogue." —*The New Yorker*

"Akhtar is a provocative, wise, and funny playwright." —Steven Suskin, *Huffington Post*

"Crackles with intelligence and behavioral truth....Akhtar is so eminently gifted in writing scenes that quake with powerful emotion." —Charles McNulty, *Los Angeles Times*

Praise for

Disgraced

"The best play I saw last year....A quick-witted and shattering drama....*Disgraced* rubs all kinds of unexpected raw spots with intelligence and humor."   —Linda Winer, *Newsday*

"A sparkling and combustible contemporary drama....Ayad Akhtar's one-act play deftly mixes the political and personal, exploring race, freedom of speech, political correctness, even the essence of Islam and Judaism. The insidery references to the Hamptons and Bucks County, Pennsylvania, and art critic Jerry Saltz are just enough to make audience members feel smart....Akhtar...has lots to say about America and the world today. He says it all compellingly, and none of it is comforting."

—Philip Boroff, *Bloomberg Businessweek*

"Compelling....*Disgraced* raises and toys with provocative and nuanced ideas."   —Jesse Oxfeld, *New York Observer*

"A continuously engaging, vitally engaged play about thorny questions of identity and religion in the contemporary world....In dialogue that bristles with wit and intelligence, Mr. Akhtar...puts contemporary attitudes toward religion under a microscope, revealing how tenuous self-image can be for people born into one way of being who have embraced another....Everyone has been told that politics and religion are two subjects that should be off-limits at social gatherings. But watching Mr. Akhtar's characters rip into these forbidden topics, there's no arguing that they make for ear-tickling good theater."   —Charles Isherwood, *New York Times*

"A blistering social drama about the racial prejudices that secretly persist in progressive cultural circles."   —Marilyn Stasio, *Variety*

"Terrific.... *Disgraced*...unfolds with speed, energy and crackling wit.... The evening will come to a shocking end, but before that, there is the sparkling conversation, expertly rendered on the page by Akhtar.... Talk of 9/11, of Israel and Iran, of terrorism and airport security, all evokes uncomfortable truths. Add a liberal flow of alcohol and a couple of major secrets suddenly revealed, and you've got yourself one dangerous dinner party.... In the end, one can debate what the message of the play really is. Is it that we cannot escape our roots, or perhaps simply that we don't ever really know who we are, deep down, until something forces us to confront it? Whatever it is, when you finally hear the word 'disgraced' in the words of one of these characters, you will no doubt feel a chill down your spine."

—Jocelyn Noveck, Associated Press

"Offers an engaging snapshot of the challenge for upwardly mobile Islamic Americans in the post-9/11 age."

—Thom Geier, *Entertainment Weekly*

"*Disgraced* stands among recent marks of an increasing and welcome phenomenon: the arrival of South Asian and Middle Eastern Americans as presences in our theater's dramatis personae, matching their presence in our daily life. Like all such phenomena, it carries a double significance. An achievement and a sign of recognition for those it represents, for the rest of us it constitutes the theatrical equivalent of getting to know the new neighbors—something we had better do if we plan to survive as a civil society."

—Michael Feingold, *Village Voice*

"Ninety minutes of sharp contemporary theatre at its argumentative, and disturbing, best."   —Robert McCrum, *The Guardian*

The
Invisible
Hand

ALSO BY AYAD AKHTAR

The Who & The What
Disgraced
American Dervish

The Invisible Hand

A PLAY

AYAD AKHTAR

BACK BAY BOOKS
Little, Brown and Company
New York   Boston   London

Copyright © 2015 by Ayad Akhtar

Back Bay Books / Little, Brown and Company
Hachette Book Group
1290 Avenue of the Americas, New York, NY 10104
littlebrown.com

First edition: August 2015

Back Bay Books is an imprint of Little, Brown and Company. The Back Bay Books name and logo are trademarks of Hachette Book Group, Inc.

The Hachette Speakers Bureau provides a wide range of authors for speaking events. To find out more, go to hachettespeakersbureau.com or call (866) 376-6591.

ISBN 978-0-316-32453-3

LCCN 2015942280

10 9 8 7 6 5 4 3 2 1

RRD-C

Printed in the United States of America

For Jim Nicola and NYTW

&

For Seth, Ken, and Dasha

FINANCE AND
THE FIGURE OF NOW

When I first moved to New York in my early twenties, my father made a deal with me: "Read the *Wall Street Journal* every day and I'll pay your rent." He and my mother—both physicians, both concerned by my obsession with the arts and what they saw as an apparent, and complete, lack of interest in the more mundane matters of the world—had concocted the plan. They knew their son well enough to know that (1) I would abide if I agreed, and (2) I would probably become interested if I spent enough time reading it.

Such has been my introduction to so much of life, on the written page first. And so it was with the world of money.

My rent was $580, a sum split between myself and my then live-in girlfriend. I read the *Journal* at the local library a few blocks away, and sometimes at home. Back then the front-page left-hand column was usually the most interesting—and best written—story in the news. My folks were right. I got hooked. That monthly check started to seem entirely unearned.

It was the mid-nineties in New York City, the moment of the first tech boom fueled by the advent of the Internet. Tina Brown had taken over *The New Yorker,* and in its pages, profiles of the financial elites seemed to sit cheek by jowl with the accomplishments of the moment's most cultured. Soon, twentysomethings and thirtysomethings would be flush with millions (and later billions). At book parties and dinner parties and openings, money and its allure were all the talk. I couldn't have known then that a permanent shift was under way. Or let me put it like this: An old American obsession was finding new and vibrant life, finding a figure and form that would make money—its exigencies, its amorality, its language, its ethos—central not only to the larger cultural conversation but to our experience of the human.

Surely money has always mattered to us. As far back as his journey through the fledgling democracy that was the United States in the early 1800s, Alexis de Tocqueville was able to see and articulate this with characteristic pith and pungency:

> As one digs deeper into the national character of the Americans, one sees that they have sought the value of everything in this world only in the answer to this single question: how much money will it bring in?

Was it ungracious of him to put it thus, or just a blunter way to say a thing we already know about ourselves? Some form of this question has long been a preoccupation for me—humanly, artistically. I, too, share this fascination with money—with its uses, with those who have it, with what the great Wallace Stevens once called the "poetry" of finance. Perhaps it's a form of vicarious living, the only reasonable pathway for an artist to accede to fantasies of power denied to her in life. Or perhaps it is the recognition that our *being-with-money*—that is to say, our living with it, individually, collectively—speaks to so much that is at the root of art's ultimate pursuit: the most hidden, the most human, the most primal. Beyond the free-market jingoism and all the ceaseless invocations of "The Economy"—as if those two words referred to some newfangled deity whose wrath we were always trying to appease—beyond all this, isn't money the site par excellence of our recurring quotidian terrors and soaring fantasies, and, above all, the everyday test of our character? And in America, money is something else as well: the metonymic complement of personal will itself, its acquisition standing in for the supreme American expression of individual vitality. In many ways, money is our central story.

The American story is no longer ours alone. Globalization has made it, increasingly, everyone's story. The socio-philosophical reasons for this are too complex, too contentious to be addressed in any direct way. And so it falls, I believe, to the artist to offer a picture of the world we are creating, a picture rich with contradiction, short on resolution. This, in any event, was the motivation behind writing *The Invisible Hand*—that of giving form to an American tale, but one unfolding on a global stage, an encounter of our national mythos with the world beyond our borders. Nick on one side, Bashir on the other. Yet in the end, both men at the heart of this drama resisted any schematic treatment of their so-called allegorical roles. A hostage thriller became an enactment (and inversion) of the Pygmalion tale and changed course again, revealing, at its close, what seemed to me an unlikely but unmistakable portrait of ourselves.

Ayad Akhtar
New York City
April 2015

PRODUCTION HISTORY

The Invisible Hand had its world premiere as a one-act play on March 7, 2012, at the Repertory Theatre of St. Louis, St. Louis, Missouri (Steven Woolf, artistic director). It was directed by Seth Gordon; the set design was by Scott Neale; the costume design was by Lou Bird; the lighting design was by Ann Wrightson; the sound design was by Rusty Wandall; and the stage manager was Champe Leary. The cast was as follows:

NICK...John Hickok

DAR...Ahmed Hassan

BASHIR...Bhavesh Patel

JAMES AND THE GUARD...Michael James Reed

A considerably revised two-act version of *The Invisible Hand* had its West Coast premiere on September 5, 2014, at ACT—A Contemporary Theatre, Seattle, Washington (Kurt Beattie, artistic director). It was directed by Allen Nause; the set design was by Matthew Smucker; the costume design was by Rose Pederson; the lighting design was by Kristeen Willis Crosser; the sound design was by Brendan Patrick Hogan; and the stage manager was JR Welden. The cast was as follows:

NICK...Connor Toms
DAR...Erwin Galan
BASHIR...Elijah Alexander
IMAM SALEEM...William Ontiveros

The two-act version of *The Invisible Hand* had its New York premiere on November 19, 2014, at New York Theatre Workshop (Jim Nicola, artistic director). It was directed by Ken Rus Schmoll; the set design was by Riccardo Hernandez; the costume design was by ESOSA; the lighting design was by Tyler Micoleau; the sound design was by Leah Gelpe; and the stage manager was Megan Schwarz Dickert. The cast was as follows:

DAR...Jameal Ali
NICK...Justin Kirk
BASHIR...Usman Ally
IMAM SALEEM...Dariush Kashani

The
Invisible
Hand

It is not from the benevolence of the butcher, the brewer, or the baker that we expect our dinner, but from their regard to their own interest. We address ourselves not to their humanity but to their self-love.

—Adam Smith, *The Wealth of Nations*

Characters

DAR—early 20s

NICK BRIGHT—30s

BASHIR—mid to late 20s

IMAM SALEEM—40s/50s

Place

Somewhere in Pakistan.

Time

In the very near future.

The play should be performed with an intermission between Acts One and Two.

Act One: Scene One

❦

A holding room. Spare. In disrepair. A table center stage. Two chairs. Along the far left wall, a small cot. And above it, a window near the ceiling. Covered in bars.

There's a door stage right.

Sitting at the table is NICK BRIGHT. Intelligent and vital.

Across from him is DAR—early 20s—a rural Pakistani who speaks English with a thick accent. He wears a Kalashnikov over his shoulder.

Dar is leaning over Nick's handcuffed hands. It may take us a moment to realize:

Dar is cutting Nick's fingernails.

We hear male voices offstage talking in a foreign language— voices to which Dar appears to be listening.

NICK: How's your mother, Dar?

DAR: Good. Good.

NICK: That's good.

Dar smiles, nervously.
Goes back to cutting.

NICK (CONT'D): So she's not too sick?

DAR: What?

NICK: Your mother. She's not too sick?

DAR: She sick, Mr. Nick. She sick.

> *(Beat)*

>> But she happy see her son.

NICK: That's good you went to see her, Dar.

Dar forces a nervous smile, checking over his shoulder as...

...the voices diminish.

Dar stops — listening.

We hear the faint sound of a door closing. Then silence.

Dar gets up and goes to the door stage right — listening.

Then crosses to the window upstage center — listening.

In the distance, we hear a car engine start up. Then drive off.

Dar returns to the table. He rests the gun against the chair. He hands Nick the nail cutter as he pulls a key and undoes one of the cuffs.

DAR: They go. You can cut. I know you don't like I cut for you.

NICK: Thank you, Dar.

The shift is palpable. Dar is clearly more at ease.

DAR: I not go my mother, Mr. Nick.

> *(Explaining, off Nick's confusion)*

>> I not go see my mother. I had plan. I not tell you.

NICK: You had a plan?

DAR: Before I not tell you.

>> Now I tell you.

>> You remember my cousin, he have farm? Potato farm?

NICK: Changez, right?

DAR *(Smiling warmly)*: You remember.

NICK: Of course I remember, Dar.

DAR: Ramzaan coming. Prices going up and up. Like I tell you.

NICK: Like they do every year.

DAR: Changez tell me good crop in Jhelum. Very good year for him.

NICK: I remember.

DAR: Changez is good man, Mr. Nick. People like him. He have respect.

NICK: Right.

DAR: I tell him what you tell me. Sell me all potato, all farmer he has friends. Give for me lowest price. I sell potato high price when Ramzaan come.

I tell him, we all share money, together.

NICK: And?

DAR *(Nodding)*: He talk to them. They don't sell potato to other. They give me.

(Quietly)

I tell here, I go my mother.

But I not go my mother.

I get trucks...

NICK: ...Trucks?

DAR: Three trucks. Drive potato from Jhelum to Multan market, highest price.

NICK: How did you get trucks?

DAR: I pay.

NICK: With what?

DAR: Potato. I had so many!

(Laughs)

After three days, potato gone.

(Beat)

Seven. Five.

NICK: Seven, five...what?

DAR: Dollar.

NICK: Seventy-five dollars.

DAR: I make.

NICK: You're kidding?

DAR: I change from rupee to dollar. Like you told me: Change all your saving to dollar, Dar. More...

(Speaking Punjabi)

...*pucka.*

NICK: Stable.

DAR *(Repeating)*: Stable.

NICK: Dar, this is wonderful news.

DAR: A lot of money for me.

(Beat)

Thank you for give me help.

Nick smiles, moved. They share a moment.

We hear sounds in the hall.

Nick quickly takes a seat.

Dar nervously takes the nail cutter, as Nick locks the cuff back onto his wrist.

Just as...

...we hear the lock of the stage right door opening.

Enter BASHIR—mid to late 20s—sinewy and intense. A human barracuda.

Both Dar and Nick visibly nervous by his sudden appearance. Dar stands. A sign of respect.

Bashir speaks English perfectly, with a working-class British accent.

BASHIR: Mr. Bright?

NICK: Bashir.

BASHIR: Been a while.

Three weeks, innit?

(Off Nick's silence)

How've you been?

NICK: Fine.

BASHIR: No complaints?

Wouldn't want to be hearing anything about how you'd been mistreated or some such...

Want to make sure everything's up to your standards, then.

(Nick's further silence)

Dar taking good care of you?

NICK: Dar is fine.

BASHIR: He's a bit of an arse-licker, in't he?

But gets the job done sooner or later.

Whatever job that may be...

(Patting Dar on the back)

I mean he's a good lad.

Takes care of you.

Takes care of his mum.

Bashir looks over and notices that a water pitcher on the table is empty.

BASHIR (CONT'D): What's this? Pitcher's empty? What if Mr. Bright needs a drink? What's he gonna do then? Dar?

DAR: I'll get more water.

BASHIR: You gonna do that?

DAR: Yes.

BASHIR: When?

NICK: It's okay. I'm not thirsty.

BASHIR: Well, see, it's the principle now, isn't it?

DAR: You want me to do it now?

BASHIR: Yes, I think I do. I think I want you to do it now.

As Dar approaches, Bashir suddenly strikes him. Viciously. And then again.

BASHIR (CONT'D): Maybe you should go back to taking care of old ladies, you fucking dog!

NICK: It's okay. He didn't mean it. Leave him alone.

Bashir turns on Nick. Just as vicious.

BASHIR: Who asked you to open your fucking gob?!
Hmm?!
Did I?!!

Nick looks down. Avoiding eye contact.

BASHIR (CONT'D): That's right. Let's have a little respect around here.
(Snickering)
I'm guessing it's not going to come as a surprise to you then that our little pissant here did not visit his mum this week. Innit?

Nick shrugs. Not making eye contact.

BASHIR (CONT'D): You didn't know that?

Really?

You had no idea he was out gallivantin' through Multan flogging potatoes?

No idea at all?

Or how 'bout this: that he walked into a Citibank two days ago—

You heard of that, right?

Citibank?

NICK: You know I have.

BASHIR: That's right. I do. I may know a few things more, too. Get ready for it:

Dar here walks into a Citibank the other day and opens an account that's got interest. Interest. Which he's been taught his whole life is against Allah's will?

You and your fucking interest eating up the world like cancer. You been teaching him about cancer, then?

NICK: I don't know what you're talking about.

BASHIR *(Screaming)*: You're a liar!!

Nick looks away.

Long silence.

BASHIR (CONT'D): Citibank's gone cold—you better hope they're getting your ransom together...or else—

NICK: What?

BASHIR: Let's just say, might be something to be gained turning you into a political prisoner.

NICK: I have no importance.

BASHIR: Man working with Bilal Ansoor? On taking water away from the people?

NICK: That's not what—

BASHIR: The fuck it's not!

NICK: I've always thought the country's too unstable to privatize water.

BASHIR: You told Ansoor that?

NICK: A dozen times if I told him once. My boss knew how I felt.

BASHIR: Your boss, Carey Martin.

NICK: Yeah.

BASHIR: At Citibank.

NICK: Yes.

BASHIR: I think you're full of shit.

(Shifting)

Wealthy American looting our country. Taking water from the people. Who knows? Might be something to be gained by giving you to Lashkar, innit?

NICK: Lashkar?

BASHIR: Blokes made the video of that journalist. Daniel Pearl.

NICK: Right.

BASHIR: Got his head cut off.

Beat.

BASHIR (CONT'D): You know your wife sent another one of those videos. Julie.

NICK: She did—

BASHIR: She keeps it together this time. I have to say, I was impressed. She's really a bit of a bird, in't she? Cute kid, too. His hair all messed up, snot coming out his nose...

Beat.

NICK: I didn't do anything. I didn't do anything to you! It wasn't even supposed to be me in that goddamn car. You thought it was my boss. It wasn't. You don't want me.

BASHIR: A bit of bad luck—and not just yours, to be honest...

Beat.

Bashir turns to Dar.

BASHIR (CONT'D): *(In Punjabi)* Bastard!

Bashir grabs Dar by the arm. And pulls him to his feet. Dragging him to the door...

Dar turns for a last lingering look at Nick before Bashir shoves him out. Bashir follows.

Alone, Nick gets up. Pacing.

When he sees something on the ground.

Reaches down and picks it up.

The nail cutter.

Nick holds it in his fingers.

Lights Out.

Act One: Scene Two

❦

Three days later. The same room. The cot is further stage left than it was in the last scene.

Nick and Bashir. Nick is handcuffed.

Intermittently—through this scene and others—we will hear a recurring distant mechanical buzz. Very faint. Coming in and out.

(The noise will not be referred to—or explained—until Scene Five, by which point the audience should have become acclimated to it, unaware...)

There is an iPhone before Nick. Playing. We hear a woman's voice. The video Nick's wife has made to plead for his life:

VIDEO: Nick is a good man. He cares about others. He volunteers on the weekends at a soup kitchen, feeding the poor. He has a young son, Kaden, who adores him. Please let my husband go. I've learned that Islam is about mercy and forgiveness—

Bashir grabs the iPhone. Stops the video.

BASHIR: Then she goes on and on about Islam, like she's got a fucking clue.

Silence.

NICK: So they were negotiating?

BASHIR: They were.

    (Beat)

    No longer.

NICK: I told you it was too much. You didn't believe—

BASHIR: That's not it.

NICK: I don't know how many times I've told you—

BASHIR: Would you just shut it for a change?

    (Beat)

    Imam Saleem got put on some list. Last week. Your State Department. The bank can't negotiate. She can't negotiate. It's against your laws.

NICK: List?

BASHIR: Of terrorist groups.

    (Bashir snickers)

    Imam Saleem's not a terrorist. Fucking irony? The Taliban? They don't like us any more than they like you.

NICK: Right.

BASHIR: Imam Saleem's a visionary. He's doing what you people always promise but never do. He took over the orange groves to the river. Put people to work. Running the schools, the hospital in these parts. Money for everything's gotta come from somewhere. You've been robbing us blind for sixty years. We're just taking back what's ours.

NICK: I haven't been robbing you—

BASHIR *(Over)*: The fuck you haven't. You know what was in the paper the other day? Your bank made four billion dollars in three months. Where d'you think all that money came from?

NICK: That has nothing to do with me.

BASHIR: The fuck it doesn't. Let me get this right. You work for the big man, Carey Martin, but—

NICK *(Coming in)*: He's not the big man.

BASHIR: Ask him for the money yourself? Least he can do—for taking his place.

NICK: I doubt he's got ten million dollars lying around—and even if he did—

BASHIR: If he's got bugger all, why's he in the paper all the time?

NICK: He's in the Pakistani papers. Not any others. Nobody knows who he is outside Pakistan.

   He's just a banker.

BASHIR: And Daniel Pearl was just a journalist.

   Beat.

NICK: Cutting off my head is not going to accomplish anything.

BASHIR: See, it's not us'd be cutting it off. We don't go in for that sort of thing. That's why we'd be giving you to Lashkar.
   (Off a thought, wryly)
   Always wondered about it, though. What's the part of you that—I mean your head's rolling around on the ground, thinking...—but what's happening to the other part of you? What would it be like being in both places at the same time?
   (Beat)
   If you find out, will you tell me?

   Long pause.

NICK: We can work something out.

BASHIR: Like what?

NICK: I've already told you. I can come up with two and a half, maybe three...

BASHIR: Your ransom's not three. It's ten.

NICK: That's insane! For God's sake, three million you can get is better than ten you can't.

BASHIR: I'm actually not sure it is. To be honest. Lashkar's been breathing down our necks. Coming in across the river. Shaking us down for cash. Who knows? Maybe we tell 'em you're a Jew, and you buy us some real peace for once.

NICK: But I'm not Jewish.

BASHIR: They're idiots. They won't know the difference.

NICK: I'm not circumcised.

BASHIR: Isn't anything can't be taken care of.

Pause.

NICK: God. Bashir. Don't be stupid.

BASHIR: Excuse me?

NICK: You've got something of value. Don't piss it away.

BASHIR: You got some fucking nerve, don't you?
(Approaching)
   You're the one's yapping that you're not worth sod all—

NICK *(Coming in)*: That's right. To them. To my company. Not worth a penny. Not now. Not after you people kidnapped me. In fact? To them? I'm actually a liability.
   But that doesn't mean...

BASIIIR: What?

NICK: That I'm not still worth something...to you. Just because you can't get what you want one way doesn't mean you can't get it another.

Beat.

BASHIR: I'm listening.

NICK: Just a month ago, I had a meeting with emerging markets at UBS.

BASHIR: What's that?

NICK: Union Bank of Switzerland.

BASHIR: Right.

NICK: Their operation is ten times bigger here in Pakistan than Citibank. I was actually in talks to leave Citibank and go to UBS. They were going to pay me a lot more money.

BASHIR: How much?

NICK: Seven figures.

BASHIR: For what? Showing greedy Pakistanis like Bilal Ansoor how to squeeze every drop of wealth out of their own people?

NICK: For my understanding of the marketplace. The market climate here in Pakistan...—Hell, Carey Martin is an idiot. I've been doing his job for three years. I'm worth a lot more to you alive than dead.

Beat.

BASHIR: How d'you figure?

NICK: I—uh—engineered a trade...that cleared the Gaznoor Group twenty million dollars.

BASHIR: The Gaznoors.

NICK: Yes.

BASHIR: You mean the Gaznoor family? Richest family in Punjab?

NICK: Gaznoor Group is their holding company.

Beat.

BASHIR: How'd you make 'em twenty million?

NICK: Trading wheat.

BASHIR: Wheat.

NICK: Yep.

BASHIR: You're talking about the food shortage.

NICK: No. This was the spring before.

BASHIR: That's when the food shortage actually began. Not this spring. Last spring. People buying and selling, fucking up the wheat supply.

NICK: You want to talk about how I made the Gaznoors twenty million dollars or not?

Beat. Bashir finally nods.

NICK (CONT'D): I recognized a systemic difference in the prices of wheat in Faisalabad and Multan. It was pretty drastic. And it had nothing to do with agriculture. It was just an abnormality in the distribution. Once I understood it, I was able to take advantage.

BASHIR: How?

NICK: By creating an instrument that made it easier for people in Multan to buy wheat in Faisalabad.

BASHIR: An instrument?

NICK: A future.

BASHIR: Future. Cor blimey. Heard of that.

Pause.

NICK: Where are you from?

BASHIR: What does that have to do with anything?

NICK: Your accent.

BASHIR: You know you've tried that before...

That shit's not gonna work on me. I know all about that stupid class they give you when you come work in Pakistan: Make friends with your captor, get him to see you're a human being.

NICK: I wasn't trying to make—

BASHIR: You really think I'm an idiot, don't you?

NICK: I don't think you're—

BASHIR: I'm not an idiot. And you best not be insulting my intelligence like that.

> For your information…

> I aced my GCSEs.

NICK: What's a GCSE?

BASHIR: You're not so clever after all, are you, Mr. Bright? GCSE's your final exam in school. You know about Hounslow?

NICK: I don't.

BASHIR: Well, you're an ignorant fucker, then, aren't you?

(Beat)

> You ever take the Tube from Heathrow Airport?

NICK: Yes.

BASHIR: You went right by my house. Had a view of the tracks from my bedroom. If I'd known you were passing by, I would have thrown something at your train, you fuck. See, I don't like you. I'll never like you. You're a heartless greedy bastard. And I think the likes a you are better off dead. You got that?

NICK: I got it.

BASHIR: So what the fuck is a future?

NICK: It's a contract to buy something. Or sell something. In the future. If sugar is cheap right now because of overproduction in Brazil or something, you can say, I'd like to keep buying a month from now, six months from now, at today's price.

(Off Bashir's interest)
    If you do, if you lock in that price, you've bought a future.
    If the price of sugar goes back up, then it's worth something.
    You can sell it to make money.

BASHIR: What if the price goes down?

NICK: You can make money a different way if that happens.

BASHIR: You can?

NICK: Absolutely.

    Pause.

BASHIR: Wheat.

NICK: Potatoes.

BASHIR: Right.

NICK: There are opportunities.

BASHIR: Twenty million.

NICK: Give or take.

BASHIR: A way for people in the south to buy from the north.
    (Beat)
        In the future.

NICK: And then we sat back and watched the money roll in.

    Bashir nods.
    With a thought.

        Lights Out.

Act One: Scene Three

❦

Two days later. The same room.

Nick and Bashir. And:

IMAM SALEEM. In a white shawl and shalwar. *Regal. With charisma to burn.*

He is articulate but speaks with a pronounced Pakistani accent.

IMAM SALEEM: When I started out in the world as a young man, it was as a journalist. Writing for the newspaper in Bahawalpur. South of Lahore.

NICK: *Bahawalpur Times?*

IMAM SALEEM: You know it?

NICK: I do. I've spent some time there.

IMAM SALEEM: That was home. Where I was raised. Where my family is from. I knew the place. I knew the people. I wrote local news. Stories I hoped would make some difference.

A village's entire year's wheat crop lost in a fire. A new technique for digging wells that made it easier for farmers to irrigate their fields...

I wrote a lot about farmers...

A child born to a sharecropper's family who had a remarkable ability in maths. Truly remarkable. That article was a success. Someone with the power to do something read it. That young boy got a scholarship to go to study in London.

NICK: Was that Bashir?

BASHIR: I told you I was born in London. Not Bahawalpur.

IMAM SALEEM: It was not Bashir. Though it could have been. He's like a son to me now. A very brilliant young man. Despite the occasional lapse. Your kidnapping, for example.

NICK: Right.

IMAM SALEEM: The one thing I couldn't write about, the one thing that really mattered, was corruption.

(Beat)

There is a road from eastern Bahawalpur to some of the outlying villages. A road that some fifty, a hundred thousand people depend on. Unusable.

Pockmarked with potholes the size of a city bus.

NICK: Nangni Road.

IMAM SALEEM: Right. Every year in local council Nangni Road was at the top of the list. Every year it was brought up in Parliament. Every year it was voted on, approved, paid for. For ten years. But the road has never been fixed.

(Beat)

I wrote the article. Told the story of where that money might have been going. My editor killed it. Of course, I was fired. Lectured about how I should know better. Two days later, my father was coming home from work. Three men ambushed him. They were riding motorcycles. They beat him to the ground with chains. My father was left on the side of the road. They told him: "Tell your son not to worry about Nangni Road. It's fine just the way it is."

NICK: Jesus.

IMAM SALEEM: For three days, he survived. Long enough to berate me for my foolishness.

(Pause)

You see, we are prisoners of a corrupt country that is our own making. But don't pretend you don't participate. You do. Of course you do. That's your job. That was Mr. Carey Martin's job. To grease the wheels, to rape and plunder our nation.

(Off Nick's silence)

I commend you for not objecting, Mr. Bright. One of the many things I never seemed to have learned: that the key to success in life is keeping one's true thoughts to oneself.

(Pause)

It was a very long path from that young man whose father was killed because of him to the person you see before you today. A long journey, but a straight one. A clean line. A clean line of outrage.

(Pause)

Are you following me, Mr. Bright?

NICK: I believe so.

IMAM SALEEM: What am I telling you?

NICK: That you kidnapped me... so you can fix roads.

Pause.

IMAM SALEEM *(Wry)*: Exactly.

(Beat)

When Bashir came to me with your idea, I was skeptical. But he made a passionate case. We have a growing annual budget. If he had a deeper understanding of the financial side of things, that would be very helpful, indeed. So...

If I am inclined to take you up on the offer, Mr. Bright, it will be as much for the sake of his education as for the prospect of the full ransom being paid.

NICK: Well, you'll have to reduce your expectations on the ransom, sir. Three million I can get. I can turn it into five. Feel confident about that. Ten? That's not going to be likely.

BASHIR: But that's what you said.

NICK: That's not exactly what I said.

BASHIR: It bloody well is!

NICK: I didn't—

BASHIR *(Cutting him off, angry)*: You said you made the Gaznoors twenty million. You could do the same for us.

NICK: I wasn't locked up, being held in some room.

BASHIR: Fucking hell...

IMAM SALEEM *(In Punjabi)*: Bashir. Calm down.
   (To Nick, in English)
      You don't have to humor him, Mr. Bright.

Beat.

NICK *(To Imam Saleem)*: You have to give me a realistic goal. Or I won't be effective. Give me something I can really work toward.

BASHIR: Fucking hell...

IMAM SALEEM *(To Bashir, in Punjabi)*: Calm down.
   (Beat)
      You are right. This is what I propose: mercy.

NICK: Excuse me?

IMAM SALEEM: You work to make your full ransom. If you are diligent, well behaved, but haven't made the full ten million in one year's time, we revisit the terms of your captivity.

NICK: Well that's not—

IMAM SALEEM: Mr. Bright. Enjoy the mercy I am showing you.

Pause.

NICK: I'm going to need things. Access to information. To markets.

IMAM SALEEM: Bashir has been looking into that. Very diligently, you will be happy to hear.

BASHIR: Can all be arranged. Through a good laptop.

IMAM SALEEM: You won't be allowed within a meter of any computer.

NICK: Fine...

(Beat)

No more handcuffs.

IMAM SALEEM: That is at Bashir's discretion.

NICK: Not acceptable. My hands need to be free. I need to be reading, making notes. I cannot work with these. They hurt.

BASHIR: Fine.

(Beat)

You get any fucking ideas? They'll be back on your wrists right quick.

Beat.

IMAM SALEEM *(To Nick)*: You are certain you can get the three million?

NICK: There's a way. Through my personal accounts in Grand Cayman.

Pause.

IMAM SALEEM: Then it's settled. We keep you alive. We treat you
well. Bashir learns what he can. You make your ransom. We
let you go.

Beat.

NICK: What's my assurance?
IMAM SALEEM: My word is your assurance.
NICK: Your word?
　　What happens when you don't like me anymore? Or
when you start having problems with Lashkar again?
IMAM SALEEM: Lashkar?
NICK: Bashir told me—
IMAM SALEEM *(Cutting him off)*: We are not Lashkar. We have
nothing to do with Lashkar. I don't want to hear that name.
They call themselves Muslims. They're animals.
NICK: Understood.

Pause.

IMAM SALEEM: When I was younger, I spent some time in Tren-
ton, New Jersey. Not far from where you went to school.
Princeton, right? Don't be so surprised. We should know
some things about you by now.
　　So much struck me about your country. The poverty.
Which I did not expect. And the fat people. But what I
found truly amazing was the lawyers. Nothing happens in
your country without a lawyer. No trust. In yourselves. In
each other. No conduct of life a man will not break. That's
what it means to be American, isn't it? Nobody's word
means anything.

Beat.

NICK: Sir, I used to read about what people in my country were doing to the Koran in Guantanamo? It disgusted me. That's wrong. Don't abuse what's sacred to someone.

BASHIR: What's your point?

IMAM SALEEM: No, I understand...

(Beat)

So tell me, Mr. Bright, what's sacred to you? Is it the lawyers? Or the fat people?

Lights Out.

Act One: Scene Four

❦

That night.

The room is dark except for the sharp streak of silver moonlight coming through the single barred window.

Nick lies on the cot, still.

Beat. He sits up in bed.

Quietly, Nick heads for the door downstage right and—getting there—kneels, his ear to the lock.

He listens for a long beat.

(We may or may not hear the faint sound of snoring wafting through the door from the hall on the other side.)

Nick looks satisfied as he stands and now heads for the window upstage center. On his way, he quietly scoops up a chair from its place at the table center stage.

Placing the chair silently against the far wall, he stands on it and peers out the window.

Nothing there. Only the faint sounds of insects at night.

Now Nick heads for his cot, carefully pushing it out of the way to expose the wall and make room for himself...

...as he pulls out the nail cutter...

...kneels and begins picking away at the mortar between the bricks in the wall behind where the cot stood.

We listen to the soft scratching sounds and watch him work.

Lights Out.

Act One: Scene Five

❦

Three days later.

The same room.

Now center stage is taken up by two tables. Both covered with newspapers, financial magazines, papers written on, etc.

At one table, Nick sits buried in the papers. And in printouts.

At the other table, Bashir is in the process of fiddling with a laptop. Loading software and installing.

Throughout the scene, we should barely register the intermittent distant buzz discussed earlier.

NICK: What about Jalalabad Concrete?

BASHIR: Not sure.

NICK: But he was sure about Srinagar Industries?

BASHIR: Imam said that's for sure.

NICK: But see, Jalalabad has the same history of price spikes whenever there's good political news for President Randani.

BASHIR: So it's prolly his. Wouldn't be surprised. Mr. Thirty Percent.

NICK: Ten. Don't they call him Mr. Ten Percent?

BASHIR: That was before he was president. Now? He takes as much as he wants. Greedy fuck's what he is. And a midget. *Chota*. That's what they call him.

NICK: *Chota?*

BASHIR: It means small. Which he is. Prolly more ways than one.

NICK: You know I've met him a few times.

BASHIR: Randani?

NICK: It's true. He's smaller than you'd expect.

BASHIR: Don't say it to his face. The man's a fuckin' sadist.

NICK: Has always seemed nice enough to me.

BASHIR: Nice?

NICK: I mean...

BASHIR: My uncle? Owned a petrol pump in Islamabad. He was a good man with a family. Making an honest living. As honest as you can around these parts.

One day, a black limousine stops for petrol...

Randani gets out. Looks around. Bastard goes inside, very nice, very charming. Shakes my uncle's hand. Takes off. Two days later, some of his men show up. Turns out Mr. Asif Randani would like to buy the station.

And not for the going market rate, if you get what I'm saying...

NICK: What happened?

BASHIR: My uncle sold it....After he lost two fingernails on his right hand.

NICK: Jesus.

BASHIR: That's how nice he is.

NICK: Well, says here President Randani's day is coming.

BASHIR: So what if it does?

NICK: If Randani is indicted, his net worth is going to take a major hit. The companies he owns will, too.

BASHIR: So what?

NICK: That's information we can use to make money. See, trading's about having an edge. Knowing something, understanding something that others haven't figured out yet.

BASHIR: An edge?

NICK: Yeah.

BASHIR: But you're reading about that in the newspaper, right?

NICK: What's your point?

BASHIR: So you're not the only one who knows it, right?

NICK: Yeah...

BASHIR: So where's the edge?

Beat.

Nick ignores the question. Noting the distant buzzing sound.

NICK: What is that sound? I always hear that...

BASHIR: Drones. Americans keeping their eye on Lashkar.

NICK: Really?

BASHIR *(Ignoring the question)*: Fuckin' nightmare with those things flying around. Everybody's always running for cover. You never know what they're going to hit.

NICK: Those are drones?

BASHIR: Yeah.

NICK: I haven't heard any explosions.

BASHIR: Then you're not listening.

Beat.

NICK: So you're saying the imam confirmed Srinagar as a definite yes.

BASHIR: And Buttee Holding Company. Don't forget that one.

NICK: Right. Buttee.

BASHIR: Imam Saleem said everybody knows President Randani owns that.

NICK: And Asmaan Textile Group. Okay. So with Jalalabad, that makes four companies. Let's start with that.

(Beat)

Can you log into the exchange yet?

BASHIR: Still waiting on that approval to go through. Waiting on calls and something or other.

NICK: Puts.

BASHIR: That's right. Puts. What are those?

NICK: Remember options to buy?

BASHIR: Yeah.

NICK: Puts are options to sell.

BASHIR *(Perplexed)*: Okay...

NICK: Look, just type those companies' names and the words "options chains" into Google. Print that out.

BASHIR: I don't get it.

NICK: Get what?

BASHIR: Why'd you be buying that stuff if you reckon they're gonna go down in price?

NICK: We're going to short those companies. Bet against them. It's how you make money off a stock that's dropping.

BASHIR: Shorting?

NICK: Yeah.

BASHIR: How do you do it?

NICK: It's kind of complicated.

BASHIR: Okay...

NICK: Little too complicated to explain right now...

BASHIR: Sort of your job, innit?

NICK: My job is to make money. You'll learn whatever you learn by watching. That's how I learned.

BASHIR: Right.

NICK: What?

BASHIR: You're all the same.

NICK: What are you talking about?

BASHIR: You always think you're better than everyone else.

NICK: I always think—

BASHIR *(Over, continuing)*: It's true.

　　You look down on me because of what I'm doing. Here. At least that's what you think. But in fact, that's not it. Not even. 'Cause the thing is? Wouldn't be any different if I was back in London driving around in some black Beemer in my Dolce Gabbanas, chasing after white girls like my school-mates. You'd look down on me then, too, just in a different way.

NICK: I think you're calling me a racist.

BASHIR: I think you're right.

　　(Beat)

　　Where I grew up? Hounslow? It's a slum, really. Where they stuck all of us. My father? Spent his whole life being stepped on, spit on by white people. Selling 'em knick-knacks, and thank you, sir, and thank you, ma'am, can I have another? I wasn't going in for a life like that.

　　(Beat)

Something I was good at in school? History. Though you probably don't believe that, neither.

NICK: I never said I didn't —

BASHIR *(Over)*: Thing is, I remember this unit we had about European history. The Spanish Civil War. All these young men from different countries running off to give their lives to fight the dictator, Franco. That's what I'm doing. That's what a whole generation of us're doing. Giving up soft lives in the West to fight for something meaningful.

NICK: Uh-huh.

BASHIR: See, the system's pants. There's no use working inside it. We gotta change the system. We gotta take it to the Man. Bring him to the ground and stomp his heart out. And you know what? If people gotta die in the process, so be it.

NICK: This? Is not helpful.

BASHIR: Of course it isn't helpful. It's nothing you like hearing, so it isn't helpful.

NICK: You done?

BASHIR: D'you know Ronald Reagan had the Taliban to the White House when he was president? He called 'em the moral equivalent of your founding fathers.

NICK: I doubt that.

BASHIR: No, he did. I'll show you. It's on YouTube.

NICK: Actually, I'd rather you pull up the options chains for the companies we're talking about.

Beat.

BASHIR: For what? For your shit idea that everybody else already knows about?

NICK: Do you have a better one?

BASHIR: You looking for an edge?

NICK: Yeah.

BASHIR: Information that no one else's got?

NICK: You have it?

BASHIR: Your best mate, Bilal Ansoor? —

NICK: He's not my best friend —

BASHIR *(Over)*: Gonna be meeting his maker in two days.

NICK: Excuse me?

BASHIR: Bilal Ansoor. Minister of Water and Energy. Gonna be hit. Lashkar's got a bombing planned day after tomorrow.

NICK: You know this? For sure?

BASHIR: Imam Saleem's not the only one who thinks privatizing water is not in the people's interest.

Beat.

NICK: We need to get to work.
  (Crumpling up the list)
      We're gonna need a new list.

Lights Out.

Act One: Scene Six

❦

Two days later.

Bashir sits at the table, the laptop open. Eager.

Nick paces behind him. Agitated.

NICK: What time is it?

BASHIR: Ten past three.

NICK: Why hasn't it hit the news yet?

Bashir refreshes the screen. And again.

NICK (CONT'D): Now?

BASHIR: Not yet.

NICK: You have the trading screen open?

BASHIR: Yes.

NICK: All five companies listed?

BASHIR: Look for yourself.

Nick peers in over Bashir's shoulder.

NICK: Good.
    (Scanning)
        Jaan Subsidiaries.
        Paani Filter Technologies.
        First Wave Ltd.

Gwadar De-Sal.

What about Kaghan Pure? Where's that?

BASHIR: Right in front of you. KPOXX.

NICK: Oh, right.

Nick steps away. Pacing.

BASHIR: What's gotten into you?

NICK: I'm fine.

Okay. Good. So those are the water concerns I know Bilal Ansoor had major ownership stakes in. I don't know if they're all exposed the same way. And he's probably got more. But that should get us somewhere.

BASHIR: So what are you worried about?

NICK: It's a fucking huge position. Two and a half million on a bunch of crappy options.

BASHIR: What's the risk? If nothing happens —

NICK *(Coming in)*: Cost of the transaction? On a two-and-a-half-million-dollar position? Significant. And that's if nothing happens. If for some reason prices don't drop but rise? We lose serious money.

Beat.

BASHIR *(Perking up)*: Okay. There it is. *Pakistan Times.* Breaking news. Suicide bombing in Karachi. Omni Hotel. Yep, yep. At least fifty injured. Water minister Bilal Ansoor reported dead.

NICK: Okay.

BASHIR: What now?

NICK: Just wait. See what happens.

BASHIR: Nothing.

NICK: Just keep waiting.

BASHIR: Not a thing.

Pause.

NICK: Those are real-time quotes, right?

BASHIR: You know they are.

NICK: Actually, I don't. I didn't set it up.

BASHIR: They're real-time.

(Suddenly)

Right, here we go. Jaan and Paani down. Jaan three, four and a quarter. Paani down two and a half. Two. Two and a half. Four. Wow. Christ, Nick. Just like that. Went down seven.

NICK: Right.

BASHIR: Kaghan, First Wave not moving. But… Gwadar De-Sal… down… wait a second… thirteen rupees.

NICK: Okay, it's not a lot, but they're moving together. Just keep watching.

BASHIR: First Wave starting to move down. Four rupees. Six. Six and a half. Ten. Kaghan moving, too.

NICK: What's the rest of the market doing?

BASHIR: Not much.

NICK: How's volume?

BASHIR: Where's that?

NICK: The last column.

BASHIR: That one?

NICK *(Approaching the computer)*: Right. Good.

They're pouring in. Buyers are coming in.

BASHIR: Kaghan down fifteen to two twenty-five. Paani down twenty-four! Jaan down forty-three rupees. Jesus. They're moving, Nick! They're moving!

NICK: Yeah, it's picking up now.

BASHIR *(Excited)*: What do I do?

NICK: Nothing. Just wait. Stay calm. Making money can get intoxicating. You have to stay sober. Bad things happen when you're not thinking straight.

BASHIR: Everything down. Dropping.

NICK: The rest of the market?

BASHIR: Steady.

(Suddenly)

Here's the first official report.

(Reading)

"Among the dead is controversial water minister Bilal Ansoor. Ansoor's death will spell some uncertainty for the large-scale water privatization that has been under way in parts of Sindh Province and which has been seen as the test model for a possible national directive."

NICK: How many people were killed?

BASHIR *(Reading)*: "Forty-five confirmed dead. Seventy-eight wounded.

"Ansoor was in attendance at the wedding of his eldest daughter."

NICK: It was a fucking wedding?

BASHIR *(Reading)*: "Ansoor's wife, the well-known film actress Fiza Qureshi, was also reported killed."

NICK *(Alarmed, quietly)*: Holy shit.

BASHIR: Fucking whore is what she was.

NICK: What are you talking about? What do you know about her?

BASHIR: She's a film actress.

NICK: Do you know her?

BASHIR: Don't have to. They're all prostitutes.

NICK: Keep your fucking ignorant opinions to yourself.

BASHIR: What's wrong with you?

NICK: She happened to be a very nice woman.

BASHIR: For a prostitute.

Nick looks over Bashir's shoulder. Stewing. Angry. Conflicted.

BASHIR (CONT'D): Kaghan dropping through the floor.

Pause.

NICK *(Decisive)*: Sell.

BASHIR: What?

NICK: Start selling.

BASHIR: But the prices are falling.

NICK: Bashir. Just do it.

BASHIR: Why? We're still making money.

NICK: Volume's dropping. It's gonna turn. Get out.

BASHIR: It's not turning.

NICK: Bashir—

BASHIR: Kaghan down another seventeen to two-oh-eight—

NICK: I understand the situation here—

BASHIR: Gwadar's still moving, too—

NICK: And I understand that I'm in charge right now. So just do
     as you're told. Sell.
     (Off the screen)
       Look. See? First Wave. Isn't moving.
     (Beat)
       Put in the order to sell.
     (Beat)
       Do it!

Bashir finally relents.

BASHIR *(Confused)*: Sell at market?
NICK *(Irritated)*: No. At the current ask.
>They'll wait to fill the orders and skim. We're selling a lot of contracts. Pennies matter.

Bashir types orders in...

Nick watching...

NICK (CONT'D): Goddamnit, Bashir! Not like that. Put the number in there.
>Look, just let me do it.
BASHIR: Get back. Now. You are not touching the computer.
>*(Back to typing)*
>In there?
NICK: Yes.

Bashir keeps typing in the orders.

Nick watches.

BASHIR: Kaghan sold. Two thousand five hundred contracts at two-oh-five.
>*(Typing, beat)*
>First Wave position...
>...closed at seventy-four rupees.
>*(Typing, beat)*
>Paani closed at one seventy-one.
>*(Typing, beat)*
>Gwadar closed at one fifty-six.
>*(Typing, beat)*
>Jaan Subsidiaries...

(Waiting)
> ...now closed at ninety-five and a half rupees.

NICK: Proceeds?

BASHIR: One hundred fifty-one million six hundred thousand forty-three rupees.

NICK *(Calculating)*: ...so we made roughly seven hundred thousand dollars.

Pause.

Bashir continues to watch the screen.

BASHIR: Prices are still dropping.
> *(Silence)*
> Kaghan down another seven rupees.

NICK: Bashir—

BASHIR: First Wave down another ten...

NICK: Bashir, look at me.
> Bulls make money. Bears make money. Pigs get slaughtered.

BASHIR: What the fuck is that?

NICK: What they say on Wall Street.
> Being a bull or a bear means you have a disciplined philosophy about the market. You stick to it? You get rich. Greed is what loses you money.

BASHIR: You think leaving cash on the table is going to make you feel better about your best friend and his wife biting the dust?

NICK: He wasn't my best friend.

BASHIR: She give you a good blow job?

NICK: This is not about me wanting to feel better.

BASHIR: Bollocks. You're fucking soft. The whole lot of you. Can't even fight a war anymore.

NICK: That's enough.

BASHIR: Send a bunch of drones around—'cause you don't have the stomach to face death yourself. Yours or anyone else's.

NICK: I said that's enough!

Pause.

BASHIR *(Back at the screen)*: Still dropping...
   (Beat)
      Gwadar's down to one thirty-nine.

Bashir's mood shifts as he sees something on the screen. Tapping...

BASHIR (CONT'D): Wait a second...
   (Clicking)
      I don't believe it...The exchange...has stopped trading.

NICK: What are you talking about?

BASHIR *(Reading the screen)*: "Trading on selected securities suspended..."

NICK *(Reading the screen)*: "...until further notice." Jesus.

BASHIR *(Reading)*: "All trading halted for fourteen companies..."
   (Searching)
      Kaghan, First Wave, Jaan, Paani, Gwadar...
      Yeah, they're all on the list.

NICK: You sure we're out of those positions?

Bashir types again. Waits...

BASHIR: Yes.

NICK: Ten minutes. Bilal Ansoor's powerful friends started losing money. And ten minutes is how long it takes them to shut down trading.

BASHIR: Pakistan.

NICK: You'd be surprised. It doesn't just happen here.

Awkward silence.

NICK (CONT'D): Don't forget to convert the proceeds to dollars.

BASHIR: Now?

NICK: Yes.

Bashir starts typing into the computer.

NICK (CONT'D): The rupee is one political crisis away from insolvency. Downward pressure on the rupee means we make money just by keeping dollars.

BASHIR *(Off the computer screen)*: Okay. Rupees converted.

NICK: Okay. Well, we're done for the day.

Long pause.

BASHIR: Well done. You got us out.

NICK: Yeah. Well. I couldn't have predicted that.

BASHIR: What a disaster if we'd been left with that stuff...

NICK: Not necessarily. I mean, they have to start trading again at some point.

(Beat)

But I wouldn't want to have to sleep on that.

Long pause.

Bashir goes to Nick's cot. Takes a seat.

BASHIR: I'm sorry.

NICK: For what? It's fine.

BASHIR: No, it's not. I was being a wanker. It's not appropriate. I saw the numbers dropping. I was getting greedy.

(Beat)

"The greedy man is like the silkworm: the more it wraps itself in its cocoon, the less chance it has of escaping."

NICK: What's that?

BASHIR: The Prophet Muhammad. Peace be upon him.

NICK: Like I said, pigs get slaughtered.

BASHIR: Not in Pakistan, mate.

(Lying down)

You're right about making money. It really is a bit like being banjo'd, innit?

NICK: Banjo'd?

BASHIR: You know. Leathered. Ripped. Arsed. Drunk.

NICK: You drink?

BASHIR: Did all that. Back home. Growing up. Don't touch the stuff now, of course.

NICK: Right.

(Beat)

Um—Bashir, you know, I don't have a lot of things of my own at this point and...well...do you mind letting me have my own bed...?

BASHIR *(Realizing)*: Right.

NICK: Thanks.

Bashir gets up. And goes to the table. Where he sits.

BASHIR: You sleeping okay on that thing?

NICK: Fine.

BASHIR: Maybe we should get you another one.

NICK: I'm fine, Bashir.

BASHIR: Something more comfy.

NICK: I'm used to it now. I like it.

Bashir nods.

Silence.

BASHIR: I know you don't get it, but sometimes the revolution is violent. And sometimes the peace can only come after the violence.

Beat.

Nicks nods. Not affirming. Not denying.

Another long pause.

BASHIR (CONT'D): I know what you're going through.

NICK: What's that?

BASHIR: Last year, my mum died. Back in London. We'd been out of touch. Seven years. My father wouldn't let her speak to me. He didn't understand what I was doing. Couldn't understand. All he cared about when I was growing up? Asking after my love life, chuffed to bits anytime he got wind of something going on with a white girl. He's a dirty old geezer and he treated my mum like shit, but she listened to him...

    A woman deserves better.

NICK: I agree.

BASHIR: Innit?

NICK: Absolutely.

Lights Out.

Act One: Scene Seven

❧

Night.

Nick is alone.

He stands on the chair, looking out the window. Taking in a scene we cannot see.

Yapping dogs in the distance.

After a long beat, he quietly steps off the chair and returns it to the table. Pulls the cot out quietly and resumes the work of digging discreetly at the wall with the nail cutter ...

Lights Out.

Act One: Scene Eight

❧❧❧

The following day.

The same room.

*Bashir and Nick. At the tables. Nick explaining. Bashir
listening and responding. Laptop open before him.*

NICK: The most important thing about money, Bashir, is that
people don't like losing it. People, companies, governments.
So they're always looking for safe places to put it. For seventy years, the safest place has been the U.S. dollar.

BASHIR: Seventy years?

NICK: Yeah, since the Second World War. Europeans destroyed
each other, destabilized the world economy. America had to
step in.

BASHIR: How'd it do that?

NICK: Most of the world's currency rates were a mess. So the
decision was made to get everyone back on gold.

    To stabilize things. But that only worked if someone
could guarantee the price of gold. Which the U.S. came in
and did, at thirty-five dollars an ounce. If France wanted
money for their gold? They came to America. Germany,
England? Same thing.

BASHIR: Right.

NICK: We guaranteed that price for nearly thirty years. Effectively becoming the world's bank.

BASHIR: Brilliant.

NICK: It was called the Bretton Woods system.

BASHIR: The what system?

NICK: Bretton Woods. It's the town in New Hampshire where they came up with this idea. I wrote my senior thesis on it in college.

(Beat)

There's a reason I keep telling you to change your personal savings to dollars.

BASHIR: Driving me nuts with that.

NICK: Yeah? Well, people in Iran who started buying dollars? Just two years ago? Have doubled their money against their own currency.

BASHIR: Right.

Silence.

Bashir gets up.

Nick turns his attention to some statements on the table.

Beat.

Bashir stands at the window, listening. The by now familiar distant buzzing of flying drones.

And then, ever so faintly—beneath the buzzing—what could be an explosion.

BASHIR (CONT'D): You hear that?

NICK: What?

BASHIR: Listen.

More buzzing. And another distant explosion.

NICK: Yeah.

BASHIR: Drone attack.

NICK: How far is that?

BASHIR: Other side of the river. Ever since Lashkar hit Bilal Ansoor, they've been feeling the pain.
(Pause, turning back to Nick)
So I've been wondering...

NICK: Yeah...

BASHIR: If people have it in their interest for a stock to go down, can't they just do stuff to make it go down?

NICK: Theoretically, yes. But the market is huge. A single player can't usually affect—

BASHIR: What's to stop them from getting together and making the price drop?

NICK: I mean, look. When I was working at a hedge fund, we'd leak word about a stock, sow a rumor, or buy a huge position just to get the market to move.

BASHIR: That's what I'm talking about.

NICK: Right. But it's a short window. The market catches on. So you can do that. And banks on Wall Street do...

BASHIR: It's what you did with Bilal Ansoor.

NICK: Well...

BASHIR: I mean, isn't it?

NICK: I didn't kill him.

BASHIR: I'm just saying: You had the information.

NICK: Fine. But see how short that window was? It was just a few minutes before the market started correcting by itself.
(Beat)

At the end of the day, everybody's self-interest works as a check against everyone else's. Shorts keep longs honest. Vice versa. That's what they call the invisible hand.

BASHIR: The what?

NICK: The free market is guided by the confluence and conflict of everyone's self-interest, like an invisible hand moving the market…

BASHIR: Hmm…

Bashir turns his attention back out the window. As Nick turns back to the statements….

NICK: Wait. Is this right? Are we missing…
(Searching more papers)
Are we missing money…?

BASHIR: Did that go through?

NICK: Did what go through?

BASHIR: Expenses.

NICK: Expenses?
I need that money to trade. That's the capital base. You people can't—

BASHIR: It's not you people. It's Imam Saleem. He needed it.

NICK: For what?

BASHIR: Vaccines. A stolen shipment from one of those pharmaceutical companies. He was gonna buy it. One hundred fifty thousand dollars is a small price to pay.

NICK: There's four hundred thousand missing. Not a hundred fifty.

BASHIR: What?
(Going over to check)
He said it would be a hundred fifty.

NICK: That's what they all say.

BASHIR: What are you talking about?

NICK: Wake up.

BASHIR: I'm sure there's a reason it was more.

NICK: The reason's as old as the fucking hills...

BASHIR: Four hundred thousand...

NICK: The money is actually worth more than that. The purchasing power. The trading power that it gives us. You need to talk to him about this.

BASHIR: He thinks I'm getting chummy with you.

Beat.

NICK: Yeah. Well. Whatever.
   (Beat, exasperated)
      Fucking ridiculous.

BASHIR: Stop being such a bitch.

NICK: I'm the bitch?

BASHIR: Little fucking whining bitch.

NICK: I'm the one bitching and moaning twenty-four/seven about how everybody looks down on me, and everyone thinks they're so much better than me...and the whole load of whiny crap coming out of you and your fucking imam? Who probably didn't even buy any fucking vaccines.

BASHIR: Fuck you.

NICK: No. Fuck you. And fuck your sleazebag Saleem.

BASHIR: Is that right?

NICK: That's right.

BASHIR: You forget where you are, Mr. Bigshot?

NICK: No, I didn't fucking forget! I didn't forget my wife. Or my three-year-old son. Or some stupid idea I had to make you fuckers money to save my life. My wife's hair is probably falling out of her fucking head right now. Kaden? He has no idea what's going on. And I have no idea what Julie is telling him. But whatever she's saying? I know he knows something's wrong. And he's goddamn right there is.

You know what else I didn't forget? Your promise to let me go. I know how much your imam hates lawyers, but when I hear about four hundred thousand dollars missing from our trading account, I'll tell you, I wish I had a fucking lawyer.

Long pause.

BASHIR *(Troubled)*: I don't know why he wouldn't tell me.

NICK *(Off Bashir's seed of doubt)*: I've been around money a long time. And I've seen a lot of things. But there's one thing that doesn't change: what money does to people. When you get a taste, you want more.

Bashir recognizing the truth of this from his own experience. Tense silence.

Lights Out.

Act One: Scene Nine

✤✤✤

The next day.

The same room.

Imam Saleem. Bashir. Nick. And...

Dar. From the beginning of the play. Looking meek, cowed.

All look on solemnly as:

*Imam Saleem peruses the folders and papers on the table.
Taking things in.*

Imam Saleem finally speaks...

IMAM SALEEM *(Warmly)*: We were very impressed with the results of this week's work. Almost eight hundred thousand dollars, hmm?

NICK: Closer to eight hundred fifty thousand, actually, after today's session.

IMAM SALEEM: Well done.

NICK: Well, I'm working very hard, Bashir and I are working very hard, to build the capital base —

IMAM SALEEM: I understand.

NICK: Do you? I mean, because my capital base is my only leverage in the market. If you dilute my cash position...

IMAM SALEEM: The health of the local children comes before any
other consideration.

NICK: I understand that, sir. But that's not actually our agreement. If you want to remove funds from the trading account,
I think we should be having a conversation about lowering
the ransom amount.

IMAM SALEEM: Nick...

NICK: Just hear me out, sir. Three and a third to one. That's what
you want me to make. Take three million, turn it into ten.
At that ratio, four hundred thousand dollars is actually
worth a million and a half. Which would mean that the
more realistic ransom number, now, after the withdrawal, is
eight and a half million.

IMAM SALEEM: I see.

NICK: Do you?

IMAM SALEEM *(Continuing)*: Can I call you Nick, or is it
Nicholas?

NICK: Whatever you want.

Pause.

IMAM SALEEM: Just yesterday, Nick...I found myself in a conversation with you. My wife thought I was losing my mind,
when she found me talking to myself in the evening.

NICK: Okay.

IMAM SALEEM: Humor me, Nick.

(Beat)

I found myself wondering if perhaps you were the sort of
person who thought religion is the opiate of the people?

NICK: That's Marx.

IMAM SALEEM: I know who it is.

NICK: I don't know why you thought I was the sort of person who—

IMAM SALEEM *(Suddenly)*: So you don't believe religion keeps the people sedated, unthinking, accepting of the conditions that oppress them?

Beat.

NICK: I...think lots of things can do that.

IMAM SALEEM: Very good answer. Very politic.

NICK: I'm not being politic.

IMAM SALEEM: I'm not sure I believe you.

(Pause)

Do you believe in God?

NICK: I'm not sure what the relevance...

IMAM SALEEM: Humor me. Please.

NICK: I guess...—Yes, I believe in God.

IMAM SALEEM: And what is your God called?

NICK: He doesn't have a name, exactly...

IMAM SALEEM: A feeling, then.

NICK: Yeah. That's right. He's a feeling.

IMAM SALEEM: And what do you do for this feeling?

NICK: What do I do for it?

IMAM SALEEM: What are you prepared to do? Do you feel any obligation to this feeling?

NICK: Not really. It's just there.

IMAM SALEEM: It's there for you, to feel at your convenience... —Would you say?

NICK: I'd just say it's there. Convenient or not.

Pause.

IMAM SALEEM: So let me ask you this: What, in your opinion, can motivate people to do the most extraordinary things? Can money do that?

NICK: I don't know.

IMAM SALEEM: What do you think? I want to know. Is money at the root of the great fulfilled lives in human history?

NICK: I guess I would say no. It's not.

IMAM SALEEM: Right. Exactly right.

(To Dar, gesturing)

As I told you.

Dar steps over and starts cuffing Nick's hands behind his back.

BASHIR *(With concern)*: Imam sahib?

NICK: Wait, what's going on?

IMAM SALEEM *(Continuing)*: You see, I believe that money is the opiate of the people, not religion. Money is what puts people to sleep when it comes to the moral dimension of life.

And the only tonic, the only remedy for this sleeping sickness of money…—Do you know what it is?

NICK: What?

IMAM SALEEM: Sacrifice.

Silence.

Imam Saleem pulls out a gun. Turns to Dar.

IMAM SALEEM (CONT'D): *(In Punjabi)* Take it.

BASHIR: What are you doing?

Dar steps forward, meekly. Hesitant. Finally takes the gun.

NICK: Did I say something wrong?

Imam Saleem gestures for Dar to point it at Nick.

Dar does as he's told. Clearly in pain.

IMAM SALEEM: One thing that has always made me very angry about Americans is the way they confuse money with righteousness. Being rich does not give you moral superiority, Nick Bright...

BASHIR: We made an agreement.

NICK: If I did something wrong, I'm sorry.

BASHIR: He's making us money —

IMAM SALEEM *(Continuing)*: Three thousand of your people are killed on one day and it gives you license to kill hundreds of thousands of our people...

NICK: We can leave it at ten million. It's fine.

BASHIR: Imam sahib.

IMAM SALEEM: And to feel so good about it. You are murdering hypocrites! And for that you deserve to die!

NICK: For God's sake. Listen to me.

BASHIR: What are you doing?

IMAM SALEEM *(Ignoring Bashir, to Dar)*: Kill him.

NICK: Dar. Please, no. Don't kill me.

Bashir approaches Dar, Imam Saleem...

BASHIR: Why are you doing this?

IMAM SALEEM *(To Dar, in Punjabi)*: Kill him, I said.

BASHIR: No. You're not doing that.

> *(Stepping in front of the gun)*
> Not now. No. That's not what you promised.

Imam Saleem strikes Bashir.

IMAM SALEEM: I changed my mind.
>   *(Beat)*
>   Move...—I said, Move!

NICK: What I made for you two days ago? I can do it again. I can. Just don't kill me!

IMAM SALEEM *(To Dar)*: Do it.

NICK: Please! No! Dar! Don't!

>   *Dar pulls the trigger.*
>   *Click. Empty.*
>   *Pulls again. Empty again.*

NICK (CONT'D): Oh God. Oh God. Oh God.

>   *Dar's shoulders collapse. Broken by the test.*
>   *Nick reels from the surge of adrenaline, terror.*
>   *Imam Saleem steps over to Dar, approving. Takes the gun.*
>   *With a kiss to Dar's forehead.*

IMAM SALEEM: Free him.

>   *Imam Saleem turns to Bashir.*
>   *Bashir can't meet the imam's gaze.*
>   *Imam Saleem looks knowingly at his charge. Having learned all he wanted from this display.*

IMAM SALEEM (CONT'D): *(To Nick)* We are expecting great things from you.
>   Just don't ever forget where you are. And who you are.

(To Dar, in Punjabi)
   Go.

Dar leaves. Imam Saleem turns to Bashir.

IMAM SALEEM (CONT'D): I'll see you at Jummah prayers.

Bashir nods.

Imam Saleem exits.

Nick looks over at Bashir. In shock.

Beat.

Lights Out.

Act One: Scene Ten

❧❧

Night.

The same room.

Nick at the wall, the cot pulled away from the area he has been working on.

He is pulling bricks quietly. One by one. A hole he has created, just large enough for him to wiggle through.

A sound outside the door.

He stops.

Listens.

Nothing.

Then back to work. Pulling the last few bricks.

With a final look around, he begins to crawl through.

The stage is empty.

Silence that lasts a long moment.

Finally, the aggressive barking of dogs in the distance.

Lights Out.

Act Two: Scene One

Ten weeks later.

A different room.

(It is important that this be very clear.)

Perhaps roomier. Perhaps more homey. Whatever the case, certainly more inhabited. Weeks have passed here, and the tables and walls are covered with the result of Nick and Bashir's work in the market: stock charts, stochastics, Black-Scholes models. Perhaps starting to appear more like an outpost conference room of some emerging market hedge fund than a captor's cell.

As lights come up, there is only Nick. Standing at a wall, with a ruler to one of the charts, making calculations and then marking the chart with a pencil.

He leans back, with a thought.

As he turns to head for the table...

...we hear metal scraping along the floor.

We realize—Nick's feet are cuffed and chained, affixed to a weight that he has to drag across the floor as he moves...

Finally getting to the table, where he shuffles through some papers and makes another note. And takes a sip from the glass of dark purple juice there. Savoring.

We hear a door unlocking and see Bashir enter from stage left.

Bashir has a large bag dangling from his shoulders.

BASHIR: Morning, Nick.

NICK: Bashir.

BASHIR: Enjoying your pomegranate juice?

NICK: How can't you love this stuff?

BASHIR: You gettin' everybody hooked around here.

Bashir is unpacking his bag at the table. All part of a routine…

BASHIR (CONT'D): You want some tea?

NICK *(Indicating his feet)*: Bashir, please…

BASHIR: Of course. I'm sorry…
　　(Toward offstage)
　　　Dar!

Dar appears at the door.

BASHIR (CONT'D): *(In Punjabi)* Unchain him.

Dar does as he's told, more reserved around Nick than he was at the opening of the play.

NICK: This thing hurts.

BASHIR: I know.

Nick stretches his legs.

NICK: You've got me locked in here. Guarded. Why this on top of—?

BASHIR: Don't start with that. You know why you're wearing it.

NICK: For God's sake, that was three months ago. I didn't get past the front gate.

BASHIR *(Firm)*: Nick.

NICK: Those guys beat the shit out of me.

BASHIR: Nick. Please.

Nick retreats. Beat. Bashir pulls a folder, checking inside.

BASHIR (CONT'D): Balance sheets you wanted.

NICK: Oh, good. You found them.

BASHIR: Took a bit of doing...—I'm going to have a cuppa. You?

NICK: Yeah. Fine.

BASHIR *(To Dar, in Punjabi)*: Bring some tea. No sugar for me. Don't forget.

Dar nods. Exits.

Nick looks down at his notepad.

NICK: So I had a few ideas last night that I want to look into this morning.

BASHIR: Sounds good.

NICK: I'll need the complete financials on these. And sixty- and ninety-day moving averages. So I'm gonna need you to hop on there...

BASHIR: Just got to get it going...
   (Setting up)
      You had breakfast already?

NICK: Eggs and parathas. Don't know how many times I've had those eggs. I still can't get used to how good they taste.

BASHIR: Nothing like an egg fresh from the hen.

NICK: And the butter. Oh, Lord.

BASHIR: I don't touch the stuff. Heart disease runs in my family. Can't remember the last time I had butter.

NICK: I pity you. The butter here is a thing of beauty.

Nick makes notes as Bashir continues setting up the laptop. Attaching a portable printer.

BASHIR *(Nodding)*: D'you sleep all right?

NICK: Fine. Though the comics kept me up late. Thanks for those, by the way.

BASHIR: I loved Archie as a kid.

NICK: Great stuff.

BASHIR: You know, I was in love with Betty.

NICK: Were you?

BASHIR: My whole childhood. And I couldn't understand why Archie wanted Veronica.

NICK: I'm a Veronica man.

BASHIR: She's a dish. I'll give you that. But so spoiled.

NICK: That's the appeal, Bashir.

BASHIR: Your wife? Julie?

NICK: She's got enough Veronica to keep me interested.

Shared chuckle.

NICK (CONT'D): Can I ask you a question?

BASHIR: Go for it...

NICK: Don't take this the wrong way.

BASHIR: What is it?

NICK: I don't want you to take it the wrong way...

BASHIR: Now I'm curious.

NICK: What's the deal with the virgins in heaven?

BASHIR: Right.

NICK: I mean...

BASHIR: To be honest, Nick, I really don't know.

NICK: I mean, why would you want virgins in heaven, right? Virgins aren't actually any good in bed.

BASHIR: Right.

NICK: I'm sorry. I didn't mean to be—

BASHIR: It's fine, Nick.

(Beat)

You know, Imam Saleem says it's a metaphor, something about going back to innocence. The pleasure of the body. When it was still pure. Still innocent.

(Beat)

For whatever that's worth.

NICK: Like Adam and Eve before the fall.

Bashir doesn't register this as he starts typing at the computer.

NICK (CONT'D): How long have you known the imam?

BASHIR: Five years.

NICK: That all?

BASHIR: When I first ended up here in Pakistan, I spent a couple of years fighting in Kashmir. In the north. Though it didn't take that long to see what a corrupt crock of shit that was. So I left that.

(Beat)

I was staying with a cousin in Attock, who kept talking to me about this imam.

NICK: Imam Saleem.

BASHIR: Right. That's how I met him.

Dar appears at the door. With tea service.

Dar serves the cups.

Bashir pulls out a copy of the Financial Times. *And tosses it across the table.*

BASHIR (CONT'D): Picked it up this morning. Article about that boss of yours on the back page. Carey Martin.

Nick takes up the paper.

NICK: What's it say?

BASHIR: He got the sack.

Beat.

NICK: Finally did, did he?

BASHIR: You saw it coming?

NICK: Incompetent. I was doing his job.

BASHIR: Well, with you gone, they figured that out.

NICK: You kidnapping me did what people in my department have been trying to get done for three years.

BASHIR: Funny how that works.

NICK *(Reading)*: "Taking time off to spend with his family." Fucking family? He's getting a divorce. His kids hate him.

BASHIR: If he was such a wanker, why was he in charge?

NICK: Get other people to do the work for you, and take credit. It's what bosses do.

BASHIR: What a boss is, innit?

NICK: There was actually an attempted coup in the department. I'd been there six months. Which was long enough to see that Martin was a moron. I didn't know this at the time... I was the hire he made trying to shore up his base of support. So everyone was suspicious of me. At least at first. But I was in tight with the Gaznoor family.

BASHIR: Right.

NICK: I'd gone to business school with Shafat. It was how I ended up at Citi here in Pakistan, actually.

So anyway, point is, my co-workers realized I was an asset. So they ended up trying to bring me in on the plan to get rid of Martin.

BASHIR: What happened?

NICK: Carey's a moron, but they were amateurs. Hadn't solidified their relationships with the higher-ups. They made their move too soon. Half-dozen people got fired. I'd basically stayed out of it and ended up getting a promotion.

BASHIR: No blood on your hands.

NICK: Never.

Bashir takes up Nick's notepad.

BASHIR: So what are these?

NICK: Just some simple options trades. Rupee-related stuff.

BASHIR: You love the rupee.

NICK: Love to hate it.

(*Beat*)

One more major political crisis—which is inevitable—and the rupee is bust. There is a killing to be made on shorting the rupee.

BASHIR: What would the play be?

NICK: Buying currency puts.

BASHIR: Puts. Right. So why don't we just stock up on 'em?

NICK: Well, trouble with waiting on a political crisis is it could take two months, or it could take two years. Impossible to hold on to a position big enough to be meaningful for an indefinite period of time like that.

BASHIR: Right.

(Beat)

Pakistanis had any sense in their brains, they'd be tying the rupee to a basket.

NICK: A what?

BASHIR: Basket of currencies.

Beat.

NICK *(Surprised)*: You're right.

BASHIR: Don't be so surprised. Got the idea from you, Nick.

NICK: We never talked about—

BASHIR *(Cutting him off)*: From your thesis. Have it on my phone.

(Pulling it out)

"Bretton Woods and the Changing Role of the Central Bank." By Nicholas E. Bright.

NICK: You have my senior thesis on your iPhone?

BASHIR: Typed your name into LexisNexis. Was one of the first things that came up.

NICK: My Princeton senior thesis?

BASHIR: Haven't finished it yet. Just started that chapter on currency being king. You know what? You should have called this thing "The Secret Economic History of the World."

NICK: It's not a secret.

BASHIR: To most people? Sure is.

NICK: And what's the secret, exactly?

BASHIR: That it wasn't military power that took over the world. It was the dollar.

NICK: I see.

BASHIR: What?

NICK: I mean, that's not actually true, but...

BASHIR: How's it not true?

NICK: Bretton Woods just laid a framework —

BASHIR: For the U.S. dollar to be at the center.

NICK: — to be the support.

BASHIR: The center.

Beat.

NICK: I get that you hate America, Bashir. But at a certain point, I hope for you that you'll outgrow your prejudices — especially when they have nothing to do with reality.

BASHIR: Nick. The dollar is a piece of paper. It's not gold. But the U.S. figured out a way to make everyone think it was gold. To treat it like gold. I mean, all those years the whole world was looking up to you — my parents' generation? They thought America was the greatest place on the planet. It was all because you made us depend on the dollar, and then you stuffed them down our throats with a smile.

NICK: Stuffed them down your throats?

BASHIR *(Ignoring, continuing)*: The blokes running the central banks, right? Those are the real power brokers. He who controls the currency controls the world.

NICK: You're completely missing the most important thing.

BASHIR: Which is?

NICK: Intent.

(Beat)

Look, were we at the top of the food chain? Yes. But for a good reason. We were the only major nation that hadn't destroyed itself in the Second World War. Europe was in shambles. If we hadn't come in...

BASHIR: What? If you hadn't come in, what?

NICK: The period of worldwide economic growth and peace after World War Two? Wouldn't have happened.

(Beat)

We were the only ones who could guarantee liquidity. You need money to get something done? We'll give it to you.

BASHIR: In dollars.

NICK: Yes. And it turns out you don't want anything else, because it's the only thing that's stable. We'll spend money on military security, and we'll even create this thing called the IMF that will help you out if you get behind. We'll create the conditions to make it all work. So that we can grow together. Countries that can't trade with one another go to war against each other. Very few wars have been fought between countries that have McDonald's.

(Beat)

Bretton Woods was actually about creating the conditions for cooperation. Growth. Peace.

BASHIR: That's what they all say, innit?

NICK: They?

BASHIR: The Spanish?

Went to the New World telling everyone they wanted to bring Christ to the heathens.

What were they really doing?

Taking gold, silver, taking land.

Then, the English?

Went all over the world, bringing civilization to the savages. What were they really doing?

Taking tea, rubber, diamonds. Taking land.

And now, America has the whole world in its hands. Wants to bring growth, cooperation, peace. With Bretton Woods. Democracy. With the war in Iraq.

But what are you really doing?

NICK: Look...

Power is what it is.

Some have it. Some don't.

Those who don't, want it.

The best the rest of us can hope for?

That those who have it will use it well.

For all its faults, America tries to use it well.

BASHIR: You really believe that, don't you?

NICK: I do.

Beat.

BASHIR: The first time I've ever heard you...

NICK: What?

BASHIR: I don't know. Express an opinion.

NICK: Yeah. Well. This is one I actually believe.

BASHIR: Guess everyone's got their version of faith.

NICK: Well...

BASHIR: I'm going to miss you.

NICK: Haven't gone anywhere yet.

BASHIR: At the rate you work? You're almost on seven million. And you know what? I'll be happy for you, when you're out of here and back home with your family.

Dar reenters and whispers in Bashir's ear.

BASHIR (CONT'D): He did?

DAR *(In Punjabi)*: What do you want me to do?

BASHIR: Keep an eye on him.

NICK: So you can get anybody's Princeton senior thesis just by typing it in?

BASHIR: Got yours.

(Beat)

It's good, Nick. You're a good writer.

NICK: I don't know about that.

BASHIR: No, you are. Made me think I shoulda gone to uni to read economics.

NICK: There's still time, Bashir. There's still time.

Lights Out.

Act Two: Scene Two

❧❧

Four days later.

Bashir and Dar stand downstage, in the middle of a conversation—an air of intrigue between them.

Upstage, the only door to the room is open. From which we may hear a few discrete sounds. Humming.

The conversation is partly in Punjabi (italicized).

DAR: *I kept a good distance from the car. He didn't see me or the scooter. They drove around for some time, then went into the city.*

BASHIR: And then?

DAR: *I lost him—*

BASHIR: *Lost him?* You lost him? How could you lose him? That's the only thing you had to do...

DAR: *Just for a little while. There were so many people in the bazaar...*—I went back to their car. And I waited.

BASHIR: *Okay.*

DAR: They came back after a few minutes, got into the car, *and drove to an office.*

BASHIR: *They?*

DAR: *He was with his wife.*

BASHIR: His wife? Imam Saleem went to pick up his wife?

DAR: *Yes.*

BASHIR: From where?

DAR: *I don't know.* But she had a bag of sweets.

BASHIR: Sweets?

DAR: Jehan Sweet Shop.

BASHIR: What?

DAR: They have very good gulab jamun there. Everybody goes for the gulab jamun.

BASHIR: Okay. I get it.

DAR: *They drove to Murree.*

BASHIR: Murree...

DAR: *They parked outside a black building.* He went inside.

BASHIR: Did he go inside alone?

Dar nods.

BASHIR (CONT'D): *What was the building?*

DAR: *Some kind of office.*

BASHIR: Office? Office for what?

DAR: *When he came out, it was with a man.*

BASHIR: *Who?*

DAR: *I don't know.*

BASHIR: *Then what?*

DAR: They went into the car, *and drove to a house.*

BASHIR: Do you know whose house it was?

DAR: *Letters in the mailbox said Khurrum Chaudury...*

BASHIR: Khurrum Chaudury.

DAR: *They went inside.* And when they came out, she didn't have the bag of sweets.

BASHIR: How long were they inside?

DAR: Thirty minutes.

Beat.

BASHIR: Who is Khurrum Chaudury? I never heard that name.

DAR: I called Rashid.

Interrupting the conversation—

From offstage, through the open door, we now hear Nick's voice:

NICK (O.S.): I'm finished. Can you unlock me?

BASHIR *(To Dar)*: Go take care of him. But wait...

Bashir takes out a thick wad of dollars. Peels off bills. Handing them to Dar.

Dar takes them. Visibly surprised. Grateful.

BASHIR (CONT'D): Don't lose him again.

DAR: Hundred dollar?

BASHIR: And don't forget: half of it's for you. The other half you give to someone who needs it.

Dar pockets the bills. Walks out.

Beat.

Finally, Nick enters. Led in by Dar. One of Nick's wrists is in a handcuff.

Nick uses a key to undo the other cuff.

He removes them and hands them to Dar.

NICK *(To Bashir)*: I was just thinking I want to go over that list of rupee-related stuff I gave you a few days ago. I want to try some of those trades again.

BASHIR: Sure thing.

DAR: I call Rashid now. Find out.

BASHIR: *You do that.*

NICK: Find out what?

BASHIR: Excuse me?

NICK: I mean—

Right.

(After Dar's exit)

So the other thing...—I want to check on that Communion Capital special dividend. See if that came through.

BASHIR: Absolutely.

NICK: You still logged in?

BASHIR: I'll do that now.

Bashir goes to the computer and types.

NICK: The funds should have hit the account this morning.

BASHIR *(Reading off the screen)*: There it is. Communion Capital. Two hundred sixteen thousand four hundred.

NICK: Good. That puts us just over seven point one million?

BASHIR: Yep.

NICK: A hundred and forty-four percent in three months. If anybody knew? I'd probably make the cover of *Forbes* magazine.

Nick peers over Bashir's shoulder.

NICK (CONT'D): Wait a second. Does that say two million three hundred thousand?

BASHIR: It's not what you're thinking.

NICK: What am I thinking?

BASHIR: The money's all there. It's just in a few different accounts now.

NICK: Different accounts?

BASHIR: Moving funds.

NICK: Why?

BASHIR: We can trade out of these, too...

NICK: Bashir. Why are you moving money?

BASHIR: Covering our tracks, Nick. Keeping a low profile. The more money we make, the more attention there is on us. Isn't anybody needs to be knowing what we're doing.

NICK: Attention from who?

BASHIR *(Off Nick's continued suspicion)*: It's all there. See:
(Typing)
   Two point seven in that account...
(Typing again)
   Two even in that one.
(Beat)
   It's all right, Nick. Really is. For the best.

NICK: As long as we can keep trading out of them, I guess I don't care.

   Pause.

BASHIR: At some point, we should be thinking about moving the money offshore. Cayman or some such, innit?

NICK: Cayman?

BASHIR: I mean that's what you were doing with your money, right?

NICK: If that's what Imam Saleem wants to do.

BASHIR: Right.

NICK: I mean, we can ask him...

BASHIR: You don't need to be bothering him about it.
   He's been a little distracted, 'f you know what I mean.

NICK: Distracted?

BASHIR: You know. Like your boss, Carey Martin.

NICK: Uh-huh.

BASHIR: Taking credit for things he doesn't do.

Just as Dar returns.

BASHIR (CONT'D): *(To Dar)* What is it?

DAR: Rashid.

Part of the following in Punjabi:

DAR (CONT'D): *That house is for sale.*

BASHIR: *The house is for sale?*

DAR: *I remember. That building the man came out of... It had a real estate office.*

BASHIR: *Real estate.* That must be why he had his wife. They must have been looking at the house. Fucking hell. What's the asking price of the house?

DAR: I'll call him back.

BASHIR: Find out.
     (Beat, then calling Dar back)
        Dar.
     (In Punjabi)
        Chain him up.

Dar returns and begins to bind Nick.

Bashir stews as he begins packing up.

NICK: Everything okay?

BASHIR: Just fine.

NICK: Yeah?

BASHIR: Good thing we started moving that money around, Nick.

NICK: Why is that?

BASHIR: Let's just say it's a good thing.

No reply.

BASHIR (CONT'D): *(Packing, to himself)* Fucking hell…
NICK: Where you going?
BASHIR: I'll be back.

Nick watches Bashir pack up. Finally:

NICK: Look, Bashir.
BASHIR: Yeah?

Pause.

NICK: Be careful.
BASHIR: What are you talking about, Nick?

Beat.

NICK: I'm just saying. Don't make your move too soon.

Beat.

BASHIR: Okay.

Pause.

Lights Out.

Act Two: Scene Three

❦❧

That night.

Outside, the sounds of a night alive with insects.

Nick on his cot. Reading a copy of the comic book —
Archie. Hands down his pants.

When there are sounds outside. Someone approaching.

Then sounds at the door. The lock loudly snapping.

The door opens, and Imam Saleem enters...

IMAM SALEEM: Nicholas.

NICK: Imam.

Nick swings his legs off the bed, the chains making noise as
he does. Bound once again by the shackles.

IMAM SALEEM: Stay as you are. No need to get up...

NICK: Is everything okay?

Imam Saleem doesn't respond. He shuts the door. And
locks it.

Looks at Nick. Holding his gaze.

Long silence.

NICK (CONT'D): Did I do something wrong?

Beat.

IMAM SALEEM: I don't know. Did you?

NICK: I mean, no. Not that I'm aware of. What's going on?

Imam Saleem walks over to the table.

Beat.

IMAM SALEEM: Do you know Abbottabad, the city?

NICK: In the north?

IMAM SALEEM: Yes.

NICK: Where they got Osama bin Laden.

IMAM SALEEM: Have you been?

NICK: Once.

IMAM SALEEM: What do you remember about it?

NICK: Army.

IMAM SALEEM: Army town. Garrison. Military academy...

NICK: That's what I recall.

IMAM SALEEM: Nothing but military. Everywhere you go. Soldiers, young cadets, retired officers.

NICK: Okay.

IMAM SALEEM: Did you think it strange that was where Bin Laden was living? For so many years?

NICK: I mean, I didn't think about it. It was before I came to Pakistan.

IMAM SALEEM: Before the Americans got him, I'd been hearing rumors—for some time—that Bin Laden was in Abbottabad.

NICK: Okay?

IMAM SALEEM: Musharraf was in charge of the country at the time I started to hear this rumor.

NICK: Pervez Musharraf.

IMAM SALEEM: General Pervez Musharraf.

NICK: Right.

IMAM SALEEM: And Bin Laden was being kept in a military town.

NICK: Being kept?

IMAM SALEEM: Think about it. The United States had been pouring billions of dollars into the country to find him. For ten years. Billions. Would you give up the very reason all of that money is coming into the country?

NICK: You're saying the Pakistanis were keeping him alive, keeping him hidden.

IMAM SALEEM: He was the cash cow. And now that he's dead? Not even half the money is coming in.

NICK: I'm not sure I like what I think you're saying to me.

IMAM SALEEM: In what sense?

NICK: You're saying I'm a cash cow.

IMAM SALEEM: That is true as well.

(Beat)

No, what I am saying is: The Pakistanis are not good partners. Not to you, the Americans. And not to their own people. They cannot be trusted.

(Beat)

It is never good when partners, who should trust each other, are hiding things from one another.

(Beat)

You understand that I am the only one who controls your destiny, Nicholas.

NICK: Of course.

IMAM SALEEM: Not Bashir.

NICK: Of course not.

IMAM SALEEM: So any cooperation with Bashir that I am not aware of—hiding money in new accounts, for example—you understand I would feel...betrayed.

NICK: As well you should.

IMAM SALEEM: And if I felt betrayed, you understand I would make you pay for that.

NICK: Yes.

IMAM SALEEM: But if in fact you were a good partner, a partner I could trust—not like Pakistan—I would reward that trust?

NICK: Yes.

IMAM SALEEM: Despite the fact that you are clearly an advantage to us, a cash cow, as you put it...

NICK: Right.

IMAM SALEEM: So is there something you would like to tell me?

Beat.

Lights Out.

Act Two: Scene Four

❧❧

Two days later. Day.

Nick seated at the table, his feet still bound to the metal weight. Dar is seated alongside him. As at the opening of the play, Dar is leaning over Nick's hand. Clipping his fingernails. But the vibe between them is very different. Dar, silent. Nick, frustrated.

NICK: I don't know why you won't tell me, Dar.

Pause.

Dar clips. Clips again.

NICK (CONT'D): Where is he? Can't you just tell me that?

Clipping. Clipping again. Ignoring Nick's inquiries.

Nick tries another tack:

NICK (CONT'D): How's your mother, Dar?

Which gets a response:

DAR *(Perplexed)*: My mother?
NICK: She okay?

Dar ignores him. Goes back to clipping.

NICK (CONT'D): Your cousin, Changez? Must be at the beginning of a new cycle for the potato crop...How is he doing?

No response.

More clipping.

DAR: Feet?

NICK: It's okay. They're fine. Do you know when Bashir will be back?

DAR: I go now.

NICK: Wait, wait, Dar.

DAR: What?

NICK: Just tell me this. Is he coming back?

Dar exits.
Closing the door behind him. The lock snaps shut.

Lights Out.

Act Two: Scene Five

❧❧

The following day.

Nick, alone. At the table. Working.

We hear the door unlocking and see Bashir enter. Looking chipper.

At first, Nick is surprised to see him. Thrown, even.

BASHIR: Morning, Nick.

NICK: Bashir.

BASHIR: Sorry about not...

NICK: Been three days.

BASHIR: I know.

NICK: I had no idea where you were.

BASHIR: I said I'm sorry.

NICK: Where were you?

BASHIR: Just taking care of some things, Nick.

NICK: I can't work if you're not here. You know that, right?

BASHIR: Of course.

>   *(Off a sudden thought)*

>   We should get that thing taken off you...

NICK: Yeah, I'd appreciate that.

Bashir goes to the door.

BASHIR: Dar! Dar!
(Turns back inside)
    He'll be right here...

Nick notices that Bashir doesn't have a bag...

NICK: Where's your computer?
BASHIR: Oh, right. Was thinking, might not be needing that right now.
NICK: Why not?
BASHIR: Figure you might be busy with some other things today...

Just as...

Dar appears at the doorway, with Imam Saleem, beaten, bloodied, bound.

BASHIR (CONT'D): Keeping the imam a little company, innit? Seeing as how you two like talking so much. Maybe you could even give him some advice on...
(To Imam Saleem)
    ...investing in real estate. That's the people's money. Not your money.
IMAM SALEEM: *You* speak for the people now? You are greedy, you are ungrateful—

Bashir hits Imam Saleem. Hard. And he collapses to the floor.

BASHIR: I'm greedy!?

Bashir looks over at Nick.

NICK: I—uh—didn't—

BASHIR *(Cutting him off)*: It's okay, Nick. I get it.

I'm just glad I didn't take your advice about not making my move too soon. I'm glad I didn't listen to you. For once.

Bashir and Dar move to exit.

But before leaving, Bashir pulls out his phone. Snaps a photo of Saleem as he passes.

BASHIR (CONT'D): *(To Dar)* Let's go.

Both exit. Snapping the lock shut.

Leaving Nick with Imam Saleem, who continues quietly to moan.

Lights Out.

Act Two: Scene Six

❧❧

That night.

Nick in bed. Not able to sleep.

Imam Saleem, lying on the floor. The wheezing sound of his breath going in and out of him making it clear his condition is deteriorating.

We watch for a moment.

Finally, Nick sits up in bed. Looking over at Saleem.

NICK: Do you need something? Water?

Imam Saleem grunts. Then begins speaking, not exactly to Nick. And not exactly not to Nick.

IMAM SALEEM: You were the mistake.

NICK: What?

IMAM SALEEM: You were the mistake.

Quiet.

IMAM SALEEM (CONT'D): Like a cancer.
   (Beat)
   He was like a child, when I found him. Like a child. Tell me I bought a house. I don't want a house.

(Beat)
    Milk for those to drink. Fire from the green tree.

Just as . . .

We hear something at the door. The lock snapping open.

Dar comes in, a kerosene lamp in one hand, a gun in the other.

Uncharacteristically vicious in his demeanor.

Barely acknowledging Nick, he sets the lantern down on the table and goes to Imam Saleem. Brusquely lifting the ailing man to his feet. Then Dar drags Saleem out of the room.

Leaving the door open.

Sounds of movement and Imam Saleem's incoherent and terrified objections . . .

Nick goes over to the window to look outside.

Gets there just in time to see—

What we will hear—

IMAM SALEEM (CONT'D): *Allah hu Akbar.*

Then a gunshot. And another.

Silence.

Dar comes back into the room.

Nick flinches. Convinced he is next.

NICK: No, please, don't, Dar. . . .

Dar looks over at Nick, heaving from the adrenaline of killing Saleem. With a chilling, inscrutable expression. By the light of the kerosene lamp, we see:

Dar's face and clothes are splattered with blood.

Dar takes up the lamp and exits. Locking the door behind him.

Leaving Nick alone. Heaving…

In his moment of terror, Nick drops to his knees, and a prayer flows out, unbidden:

NICK (CONT'D): Our Father, who art in heaven, hallowed be thy name; thy kingdom come; thy will be done, on earth as it is in heaven…

Broken.

Lights Out.

Act Two: Scene Seven

Nick alone. Disheveled. He has been on his own now for three weeks.

He sits on the bed, disoriented.

He walks over to the wall. And pulls the rest of the papers down. Throwing them about.

Out of breath.

When we begin to hear the very distant sounds of gunfire.

An explosion.

And then more gunfire. The countryside awash in sudden violence.

Nick arrested, listening.

Lights Out.

Act Two: Scene Eight

❦

The same room.

Two days later.

Papers still strewn about.

Nick, eating voraciously.

Bashir stands watching him, newspaper folded under his arm. He is arrayed in resplendent robes reminiscent of those we saw on Imam Saleem. He has a new bearing, a new confidence and charisma.

We are listening to the continuing sounds of distant gunfire. The sounds of war.

Dar stands stoically guard, covered in ammunition-filled belts and holding a Kalashnikov.

BASHIR: There is blood in the streets. The city is on fire. Fighting even as far outside as across the river.

Nick drinks. Swallowing down. Out of breath.
Then looks at Bashir.

NICK: Please. Bashir. Please.
BASHIR: What's that?
NICK: I know...

BASHIR: What do you know, Nick?

NICK: I know you don't owe me —

BASHIR: Owe you?

NICK: Let me get back to work. Please. I've been in here by myself for three weeks. I can't...anymore...Let's come to some kind of an agreement.

Bashir approaches. Tosses the paper down on the table before him:

NICK (CONT'D): What is it?

BASHIR: Last Friday's paper. The story on the right-hand side.

NICK: What's it say?

BASHIR *(Picking up the paper again)*: It says that at the annual meeting of the central bankers of Pakistan on Thursday, a van filled with explosives drove into the bank and detonated, killing the governor of the state bank and all the members of its board...

(Beat)

It says the Pakistani rupee has gone into a free fall.

(Beat)

Remember how you were always saying the rupee was one crisis away from insolvency?

(Pointing at the paper)

Well, there's your crisis.

NICK: Why are you telling me this?

BASHIR: I invested all the capital we made into put options on the idea that the Pakistani rupee was going to drop in value...

NICK: You shorted the rupee?

BASHIR: And then I arranged the bombing of the central bank of Pakistan during their policy meeting.

NICK: You did what?

BASHIR *(Over)*: And now that the rupee's collapsed, my position in the market's worth thirty-five million dollars.

(Beat)

You have any idea how much good this is going to do?

(Pointing to the paper)

It's going to bring down the government. The time is ripe for revolution. Spring has finally come to Pakistan.

NICK: You killed all the central bankers...

BASHIR: Ever since that thing with Bilal Ansoor—him getting hit by Lashkar, and the window that gave us on the market—seven hundred thousand dollars in ten minutes...And then, all your pestering about the rupee—well, it finally caught on at some point. He who controls the currency controls the power, Nick. Currency is king. You taught me that.

NICK: No...God...I didn't, uh...

Nick takes up the paper, the truth slowly coming into full focus.

BASHIR: Don't worry. Still no blood on your hands.

Pause.

NICK: Bashir. Please. Let me get back to work. I need to be working. I can't...Please. Bashir...

Beat.

BASHIR: There must be some version of that Stockholm thing, just the other way around, if you know what I mean. Not you feeling things about me, but me feeling things about you. I think I got something like that.

(Beat)

Way I see it, you've more than made your ransom. I'm guessing, in my shoes maybe you wouldn't do the same, but...—You're a free man, Nick.

Bashir gestures to Dar to unlock the shackles.

BASHIR (CONT'D): *(Pointing to the open door)* You're free to go.

Bashir pulls out a wad of money, peels off bills and drops them.

BASHIR (CONT'D): Just be careful out there. There really is blood flowing in the streets.

Bashir and Dar make their way to the door and exit. Leaving the door open behind them.

Sounds of distant warfare punctuate the silence.

As we are left with Nick.

Alone.

A free man.

Paralyzed.

Lights Out.

AN INTERVIEW WITH
AYAD AKHTAR

Ayad Akhtar talks with Anita Montgomery, literary manager and director of education at ACT Theatre in Seattle, where *The Invisible Hand* opened in September of 2014.

AM: *I read somewhere that you grew up in Milwaukee and that yours was one of the only Muslim families in your community.*

AA: On the west side, in the suburbs, yeah. When we moved there, I don't believe there was anybody else, as far as I know. We certainly didn't meet anybody. We were the first.

AM: *I wonder whether that caused you to run toward or away from your religious identity as a child.*

AA: I think as a kid it probably made me run toward it, in a way, because there was a recognition, or I understood that in some way I was different. I think the way I came to formulate and understand what that difference meant was through religion. And the difference was not necessarily a bad thing; in its own way it was good because my religion was good. That was the sort of child logic, if you will. It's something you see in a lot of young, early prepubescents, a kind of flowering of the devotional. A preoccupation that seems to either prefigure or coincide with the development—the hormonal changes—that are happening in the body. I went through a very strong interest in the Quran and in tradition, to the confusion of my parents, who were not particularly religious at all. I had to seek that information out elsewhere because they didn't really care or know much about it.

AM: *I just finished reading your novel,* American Dervish, *a little while ago, and it sounds very much like your young protagonist Hayat's dilemma.*

AA: Absolutely. Hayat's trajectory is something that is patterned on my own. We're not the same person but I am certainly taking elements of my own experience and using them to give Hayat's journey life and authenticity.

AM: *Did your parents take you to the mosque?*

AA: Sometimes. I had to pester my dad. He would take me every now and then but I really had to pester him to do it. It was kind of an inconvenience and didn't happen very often, so it ended up being a special thing. Sometimes my dad would go and sit with me, but he couldn't tolerate any of the stuff that was being said. I remember he and I would get into arguments and I would say, "Why aren't you a good Muslim?" and "Why don't you listen?" And he, to this day, has never let me live that down. He's like, "You know, you were so preoccupied by that stuff. You know what you used to make me do at the mosque?" I say, "Dad, Dad, I know, you told me a bazillion times already. Please, forgive me."

AM: *Well, there's something very theatrical about a mosque, or a church, you know?*

AA: Absolutely. And, you know, I really think that my attention to the living word, spoken in public—which, to me, is what theater is—began there. With my rapt attention to what was being said at the mosque. There's a pageantry, a theatricality to it, and, interestingly enough, in Muslim tradition there's a kind of soberness to all of that, too. Which I think informs my aesthetic. You're really the first person to even bring this up. I think that there is some very deep source of my own sense of theatricality that goes back to my experiences as a young boy in the mosque.

AM: *Did you find with your friends as a young person that this somehow separated you, or did you feel as though there was a place you could put your faith, and then there was your other life? How did you incorporate the two?*

AA: My experience was that it brought me closer to others. And that's because I understood what kids were doing when they were going away on retreats with the Catholic church or Lutheran church or when kids were talking about Sunday school. It was a shared universe. In Islam and Christianity there are a lot of figures that overlap. But there was something about the devotional mind-set of religion being important. That was innate to me. A kind of love that shows up in *American Dervish,* that very pure love of whatever the mystery is that the divine stands in for—that has always been first and foremost with me.

AM: *You've referred to yourself as a cultural Muslim—is that what you mean?*

AA: Well, no. What I mean when I say that is . . . You know, a lot of Muslims and non-Muslims wonder, "Well, so, do you pray five times a day? Do you do the fast thing? Do you do this? Do you do that?" and whatever, and at the end of the day, my answer to those questions is no. My childhood faith, my literalist belief in the childhood version of my faith, died in my late adolescence. And with that died any pretension of Islam's exclusivity on the truth. It came to feel increasingly absurd to me that who you were born to and what part of the planet you were born on somehow determined the likelihood of your so-called salvation. It just seemed patently absurd. I went through that traditional awakening from the slumber of childhood faith, if you will, that so many thinking individuals go through. And I was a militant agnostic for some years in college. And then, on the other side of that, my essential devotional nature reemerged. But this time it emerged in a nondenominational form. The practice of particular rites and rituals was not meaningful to me because it was not about my experience; it was really more about the performance of those things.

AM: *It sounds as though you are still a deeply religious person.*

AA: I do consider myself a very religious person, actually, but I have my own relationship to it. It's not about the Prophet, or what language you speak when you speak to the Lord, or whatever. And that's why I call myself a cultural Muslim in the sense that I'm not disavowing my Islamic origins; I'm not disavowing the way in which it has been an important foundation for my life. I consider myself to be part of the community.

AM: *What drew you to the theater and then to writing for the theater? When did that shift begin to happen?*

AA: Up until high school there'd always been an assumption that I would just become a doctor. You know, both my parents are doctors. But I had a teacher when I was fifteen who really changed my life when she exposed me to literature and made me read all kinds of stuff. She was the first person who ever got me reading plays. She made me read Beckett and Ionesco and Dürrenmatt and Jean Anouilh and Jean-Paul Sartre. I spent two years reading everything on her shelf. I went to the Milwaukee Rep and saw some great shows. Something about it felt natural. In retrospect, I feel like I've always been sensitive to experiences that lend themselves to dramatic form.

AM: *And then you really dove into the theater in college?*

AA: In college, I started acting. I had a friend who was a director and he made me audition for a play, and it turned out I had a knack for it. I got really interested in Jerzy Grotowski and Andre Gregory after seeing *My Dinner with Andre*. Then I found myself, crazily enough, working with Grotowski for a year right out of college. Then I came back to New York and started working with Andre Gregory! I was just very fortunate to meet these very, very central, pivotal people along the path. My path into theater, oddly, has been very blessed, even though it hasn't been public for most of my life. I've been around theater since just after high school. I taught acting for ten years in New York, worked with a lot of wonderful actors, and continued to teach acting in Europe. And though I was writing novels and writing screenplays, I always knew I would write a play someday. I was gathering kindling and the igniting spark hadn't come along yet. And then it did, and I was in my very late thirties at that point.

AM: *And the spark really ignited.*

AA: Yes. I wrote drafts of four plays back-to-back in somewhere between eight and ten months. *The Invisible Hand* was the second one. *Disgraced* was the first.

AM: *And then* The Who & The What?

AA: Then *The Who & The What*. And then a fourth play which I don't really show anybody, or I haven't shown anybody yet, so.

AM: [laughs] *Eight months!* And *this enormous creative outpouring.*

AA: Yeah. They'd been gathering in me for a long time, I think.

AM: *Do you see these plays as a kind of a progression?*

AA: Yeah, absolutely. You can actually see *American Dervish, Disgraced, The Who & The What,* and *The Invisible Hand* all as movements, parts of the same gesture. And I have three more works that come from this vein of inspiration. So when I finally get through them it'll be seven pieces.

AM: *That's an extraordinarily ambitious output, and a sort of August Wilson–like trajectory of interconnected stories.*

AA: I think it's going to be three books, three plays, and a film. But that will be the body of work that sort of tries to give voice to this question of Western identity and Muslim identity for people who are living here.

AM: *Let's talk about* The Invisible Hand *a little more. This play is certainly your most overtly political. I read somewhere that you wrote a novel—or you were writing one for about seven years—about a poet working at Goldman Sachs.*

AA: [laughs] Yes. Yes.

AM: *It would seem that you've had a longtime fascination with Wall Street and the effects of the market.*

AA: Absolutely. As somebody who wishes to sort of understand the world better, I think that, in our day and age, not to understand how deeply finance has informed and defined our relationships—not only to each other but to ourselves—is to miss an important part of what it means to be alive right now, in this civilization. So that's been a long-standing preoccupation for me. I have various zones of obsession and interest: Psychoanalysis has long been one of them, religious traditions have been another, finance has been another. And all of these are just modalities of trying to understand what it means to be human at this particular moment in our evolution or being as a civilization. So, to me, the play emerges, along with one of the two novels that I am in the process of writing, as a part of this larger inspiration. The novel is set in the financial world and deals with the second-generation Pakistani-Muslim immigrant community. Somebody who grows up to make a tremendous amount of money in the world of finance and lives out the paradigm of the self-made man. But it turns out he was cheating to get ahead, which is what finance has become. That's an important issue. Power, money, cheating. American obsessions. You go back to Tocqueville and see that that's at the heart of whatever our national identity really is. And so being interested in that is just, I think, de rigueur for somebody who's interested in understanding America.

AM: *Well, in this play you give, in a wonderfully compelling, active fashion, a real lesson in how the market works. I think that a lot of people do not understand the market in this country. I read an article a little while ago about high-speed trading. I had no idea that that was happening. And I think the first time I heard about "futures," I thought,* What the heck is that? *It's all smoke and mirrors, you know?*

AA: Yeah. It's true. And I think that I'm an artist who definitely takes very seriously that dictum in Horace's "Ars Poetica" that the purpose of art is to delight as well as to instruct. And I think that is the deepest pleasure our audiences experience. You see this now with cable TV, where you have these long-form series that are often set in these interesting worlds, and part of the pleasure of the series is seeing and understanding and learning about a whole swath of American activity. Whether it's *Mad Men* or *The Wire* or whatever it may be, it's this articulation of the structure of the world, which isn't about anything didactic. It's about opening horizons of consciousness for the audience, which is what art is ultimately supposed to do. And I think it scares a lot of writers to do that, because there's a prevailing prejudice against being perceived as somehow didactic. But if you can do it in a delightful way, it leads to some very, very, profoundly satisfying theatrical experiences.

AM: *Who do you write for? Who's your audience?*

AA: When an audience begins to sense that they're being told a story, there is a kind of a waking up that happens, a very simple kind of "Oh, what's gonna happen next?" feeling. And that feeling is very similar to the feeling that I think children have when they're hearing a story. It's very clear when a child gets bored or has lost confidence that what happens next is going to be interesting or plausible. There's a sacred trust built on a narrative bond between the audience and the writer and the artist. It's something I can track in myself by seeing if I am paying attention. And so, in a way, I'm writing with an almost childlike openness in myself to the question of, "Do I care what happens next?" That simple attention, that sense of being interested at every moment. It's what I believe I share with everyone in the audience. We all have it. Strange as it may sound, that's what I would call my audience.

ACKNOWLEDGMENTS

The realization of a play in its final script and stage embodiments is the work of so many. First and foremost, the directors with whom I worked so closely: Seth Gordon, Ken Rus Schmoll, and Allen Nause. The inimitable Jim Nicola provided the lightning spark of inspiration—and unending support—that helped the play find its fullest and final form. Judy Clain, Terry Adams, Nicole Dewey, and the whole gang at Little, Brown made this edition possible. And of course none of it would have happened in the first place without my extraordinary team: Marc Glick, Chris Till, and Donna Bagdasarian.

I have benefited from the insights and talents of so many actors over the course of the writing of this play: Bhavesh Patel, John Hickok, Ahmed Hassan, Michael James Reed, Michael Schantz, Babak Tafti, Michael Esper, Ajay Naidu, Amir Arison, Debargo Sanyal, Reed Birney, Arian Moayed, Larry Grimm, Behzad Dabu, Reg Rogers, Rufus Collins, Nick Choksi, Dan Weschler, Ryan Melia, Arya Shah, Alex Gurary Falberg, Demosthenes Chrysan, Connor Toms, Erwin Galan, Elijah Alexander, William Ontiveros, Usman Ally, Justin Kirk, Jameal Ali, Dariush Kashani.

Acknowledgments

There are so many whose support and guidance were instrumental at every stage of development: Steve Klein, Shane Le Prevost, Dasha Epstein, Linda Chapman, Don Shaw, Kurt Beattie, Shazad Akhtar, Madani Younis, Amanda Watkins, Johanna Pfaelzer, Len Berkman, Kimberly Senior, Dan Hancock, Elise Joffe, Stuart Rosenthal, Mark Clements, Lucie Tiberghien, Nicole Galland, Oren Moverman, Michael Pollard, Andre Bishop, Paige Evans, Jack Doulin, David Van Asselt, Vinay Tolia, James Lapine, J. T. Rogers.

Finally, the wonderful and supportive staffs at the three theaters where this play was birthed: the Repertory Theatre of St. Louis, ACT Theatre in Seattle, and New York Theatre Workshop.

ABOUT THE AUTHOR

Ayad Akhtar is a screenwriter, playwright, actor, and novelist. He is the author of a novel, *American Dervish,* and was nominated for a 2006 Independent Spirit Award for best screenplay for the film *The War Within.* His plays include *Disgraced,* produced at New York's Lincoln Center Theater in 2012 and on Broadway in 2014 and recipient of the 2013 Pulitzer Prize for Drama, and *The Who & The What,* also produced at Lincoln Center Theater, in 2014. He lives in New York City.